Dalton's Bluff

Dalton is facing the noose when a lucky break gives him a chance of freedom. He adopts a dead man's identity, but quickly discovers he's made a bad choice when he finds his namesake had been hired to lead a wagon train of settlers on a perilous journey to their new life.

Dalton must become the guide the settlers want him to be although he had no knowledge of the terrain or the dangers lurking ahead. And as if that wasn't bad enough, the notorious Spitzer gang is on their trail, a mysterious stranger may know his identity and one of the settlers is a killer.

With the odds so stacked against him, can Dalton pull off the greatest bluff of his life?

Dalton's Bluff

Ed Law

A Black Horse Western

ROBERT HALE · LONDON

Typeset by
Derek Doyle & Associates, Shaw Heath.
Printed and bound in Great Britain by
Antony Rowe Limited, Wiltshire.

CHAPTER 1

'Keep moving,' Deputy Vaughn demanded. 'That noose is waiting for you in Applegate.'

Dalton bit back an oath and kept his fevered gaze on the river, now just a quarter-mile away. With his hand-cuffed hands held before him and the rope around his waist tugging him on, he staggered another pace. He'd been walking since first light and now his gait was more the process of him throwing out his legs and stopping himself from falling rather than walking.

For the tenth time in the last few minutes Dalton scraped his rough tongue over his blood-encrusted lips and dreamed of thrusting his head beneath the water and drinking until either he drowned or the river ran dry.

But the river might as well not be there.

Even when he reached it, Deputy Vaughn might not let him drink. The lawman could continue his relentless jour-ney through the water, but keep Dalton's rope under such a tight rein he wouldn't be able to lower his head to drink.

So, with more hope than confidence, Dalton imagined tasting the sweetness of the cool water and, as he closed his eyes and dreamed of the relief that'd bring, he stumbled. His ankle turned and he fell to his knees.

As Dalton was already at the furthest extent of Vaughn's rope, the loop around his waist yanked him forward and ploughed his chin into the dirt then dragged him on. Vaughn grunted, Dalton's weight pulling him back and halting him. Then he hurried his horse on.

On his chest, Dalton scraped across the ground, squirming as he fought to regain his footing. But with his hands cuffed together, he couldn't get leverage on the ground and he bumped and scraped over rocks.

If Vaughn had stopped for just a few seconds, he could have stood, but it was a full minute before he managed to roll on to his side and gain enough traction against the ground to climb to his feet.

When he was walking again, Vaughn used his bulging canteen to swill out his mouth and spit to the side. Then he provided a sly smile, perhaps suggesting that Dalton's stumble had encouraged him to start devising a new punishment, but then he snapped round to face the front.

Dalton resumed his steady stagger forward and fixed his gaze on the river, willing Vaughn to stop there. But then Dalton noticed why Vaughn had turned. They wouldn't be the only people by the water.

A sole rider stood sideways to them. He was watching their approach on the edge of the river with the water lapping at his horse's hoofs.

Dalton's heart lurched. This man was the first person he'd seen since his capture and his presence surely meant that Vaughn would have to let him drink.

Vaughn leaned forward in the saddle to consider the man. Dalton could by now read the varying degrees of Vaughn's bad moods from the set of his back and he judged him to be on guard for potential trouble from this man. But Vaughn needn't have worried. The man hailed them.

Vaughn hailed him in return, offering his name and learning that the man they were approaching was John Stanton. He continued at a steady pace towards him. Twenty yards before him, he halted.

Dalton carried on walking, heading past Vaughn to ensure he got as close to the water as possible, hoping that while John was watching them, he might reach an outlying puddle. But Vaughn drew in the rope, halting him at his side.

Dalton swayed to a halt and tore his gaze from the inviting water to consider John. He was thickset, his buffalo-hide jacket and the furs slung over his horse suggesting his line of business. And the firm-set jaw and steely eyes that glared at Dalton suggested he enjoyed solitude and would take no nonsense from any man.

'What's he done to deserve this?' he asked, his upper lip curled back in a sneer.

Vaughn snorted a laugh. 'Don't know where to start answering that. He's a violent critter and that's a fact. But when I get him to Applegate, he'll pay for the trouble he's caused.'

John narrowed his eyes as he looked Dalton's form up and down.

Dalton chose that moment to plant his feet wide, hunch his shoulders some more, and let his parched mouth drop open, trying to appear as pathetic as he could.

'He don't look like trouble,' John said. 'He looks half-dead. You giving him food and water?'

Vaughn bent at the waist to spit on the ground.

'No point wasting that on a man who'll swing in a few days.'

John provided a sharp intake of breath. 'Ain't telling you your job, but he should still get water or he won't live long enough to pay for whatever crimes you reckon he's done.'

'What's that got to do with you?'

John raised his eyes to consider Vaughn.

'Nothing. I just don't like to see anyone suffer.'

'Tell that to the family and friends of the man he killed.'

John looked away to point across the river, the determined swing of his head appearing to dismiss the issue of Dalton's brutal treatment from his mind.

'Anyhow, as you're heading to Applegate, if you see a wagon train heading this way I'd be obliged if you'd tell them I'm still waiting for them.'

Vaughn's shoulders relaxed with John's less confrontational attitude.

'Been waiting long?'

'Two whole days.' John nodded towards the distant mountains, their jagged outlines blue and faint in the afternoon heat haze. 'They're heading to the other side to start a new life, but I'm getting to think they might have started it without me.'

Vaughn looked at the mountains. 'There's good land over there, then?'

'Yeah, land aplenty and valleys galore for anyone to start a new life.'

'I'll remember that.' Vaughn stretched. 'But I reckon I'll rest up first. Been travelling a while.'

Vaughn swung out of the saddle, still clutching Dalton's

rope, then placed the rope on the ground. He rooted around and found a forked twig, which he pushed into the ground over the looped end of the rope.

'That twig is to secure you,' he said, turning to Dalton. 'If you dislodge it, you know what you'll get.'

And with that taunting promise made, Vaughn chuckled to himself then led his horse down to the river.

Dalton shuffled after him, but Vaughn had ensured that the maximum extent of the rope would stop him ten yards from the river. He halted and watched Vaughn water his horse while keeping his back deliberately turned, goading Dalton into disobeying him and giving him a chance to administer yet another beating.

The hot sun beat down on Dalton's bowed back as he glanced at John, but he'd already turned away to stare across the river, looking out for the wagon train. Dalton dismissed his last lingering hope that this man might help him and stared at the water. He rasped his tongue over his lips as he weighed up the pleasure of gulping several mouthfuls of cool water against the pain of the beating that would follow. The water won.

He rolled his shoulders and settled his stance, practising the actions that'd let him gulp down the most water in the shortest possible time. Then he ran with all his strength, pounding the ten yards in a few long strides, and hurled himself to the ground, sliding on his belly until his head dunked into the edge of the river. He buried his face in the coolness and gulped.

Vaughn had denied him sustenance for so long that after his first gulp, nausea clutched his throat and he dry-retched. But then he gulped again and dragged water into his empty stomach.

He heard Vaughn shouting at him, his tone both annoyed and delighted with Dalton's defiance, but Dalton was counting the gulps. He'd hoped to get three swallows down before Vaughn stopped him, but he'd managed five before a hand slammed on his back and bodily lifted him from the ground before setting him down on his feet.

With his eyes closed, Dalton threw back his head and let the water in his mouth seep down into his grateful guts, then looked at Vaughn. But it was to see a pile-driving blow crunch into his cheek. Dalton was so weak he collapsed, but he got lucky.

He was still standing beside the river and the blow rolled him into the water. He came to rest on his belly and thrust his head below water then slurped in another gulp before Vaughn pulled him up. This time, he dragged Dalton away from the river before throwing him to the ground.

And then he started to punish him, whipping him with the knotted end of the rope. Stinging blow after stinging blow rained down on Dalton's wet back as he tried to escape from them, but no matter in which direction he crawled, they continued to hammer down on him.

But then the blows stopped. The beatings had never stopped that quickly before and Dalton steeled himself for the next round of brutalizing, but instead, he heard John speak.

'Stop beating him,' he ordered.

'I'll do anything I want to my prisoner,' Vaughn snapped, then paused letting Dalton hear John grunt his disapproval. Vaughn lowered his voice. 'Do you want to know what he did?'

'Nope. That man may be the most evil critter who ever

lived, but you got no right beating him for drinking water.'

Vaughn snorted as Dalton rolled on to his side and looked up. Vaughn and John were facing each other ten paces apart with their feet set wide and their shoulders hunched.

'Obliged,' Dalton croaked. 'And I ain't no evil man. I didn't do—'

'Be quiet,' Vaughn roared, swirling round. He advanced on Dalton with his fists raised, but then stomped to a halt and straightened. 'I got fine hearing, John, and that had better not be a gun you've just drawn on me.'

Dalton crawled to the side to see past Vaughn and saw that his captor was right. John *had* drawn a gun and had aimed it squarely at Vaughn's back.

'Seeing as how you can't deliver a man to justice without treating him like an animal, I reckon as I'll take custody of him.'

'You won't. You'll lower that gun, and then me and my prisoner are leaving.'

'That ain't happening. I could do with visiting Applegate to see what happened to the wagons. And while I do that, I'll see he gets to a decent lawman like Sheriff Melrose.'

Vaughn flexed his shoulders, his face darkening, his fists opening and closing.

'I'll give you no trouble,' Dalton shouted, 'if you treat me fairly. I reckon I can answer the charges against me.'

Vaughn flared his eyes, as Dalton knew he would any mention of the fact that Dalton wasn't a cold-hearted killer always sent him into an uncontrollable rage.

Then Vaughn threw his hand to his gun and turned at the hip, his gun clearing leather as he swirled round to aim at John using the same lightning speed that had captured Dalton earlier.

But John was aware of the possibility of Vaughn turning on him and he fired.

Two simultaneous crisp shots destroyed the quiet of the hot afternoon. Then Vaughn and John stood still, staring at each other, smoke rising from the barrels of both their guns. John stood square on, facing Vaughn, who stood twisted.

The motion of both men had been so quick that Dalton was unsure whether either man had hit the other, but then he saw John straighten up, his hand shooting up to clutch his chest beneath the heart. Then he keeled over, his face burying itself in the dirt.

Dalton closed his eyes a moment, then darted his gaze to Vaughn, who was still half-turned away from him, his stance frozen as he watched John's twitching form.

But then Vaughn stumbled a pace. His legs buckled and he came tumbling down to collapse on his side. Dalton couldn't help but deliver a whoop then hurried to Vaughn's side and threw him on his back.

He knew the precise location of the keys to his handcuffs. He thrust one hand into Vaughn's jacket and tore the gun from Vaughn's limp grasp with the other. The key emerged coated in blood.

Dalton danced back, his gaze fixed on Vaughn, still unsure as to whether his captor was dead but ensuring he gained as much as he could from the situation.

He jabbed the key into the lock, heard the handcuffs spring open, then shrugged them away. Then, with his hands free, he struggled his way out of the rope to stand free for the first time in two weeks.

'Vaughn,' he grunted, turning the gun on the lawman, 'things have just changed around here.'

He glared down at the deputy sheriff, but the man was oblivious to Dalton's demand as he twitched then stilled. Dalton continued to watch him, seeing that Vaughn still lay supine, then paced to his side and kicked him in the chest, but received no complaint. He watched Vaughn's head loll so that he pressed a cheek into the dirt. And his open mouth didn't move the dirt before him.

With only the slightest of cheer in his heart, Dalton accepted that his cruel tormentor was dead, but he still kept one eye on him as he hurried over to join John. He hunkered down beside him and rolled him on his back. Although John's eyes were open, they were glazed and his breathing was shallow.

Dalton had little knowledge of doctoring but he guessed that water might help. He turned to go to the river, but John threw out a hand and grabbed the trailing end of his jacket.

'Stay,' John grunted. 'He got me with a good shot. Must have slowed up.'

'I'm obliged.'

John winced, his body racking backwards, then he fixed Dalton with his steely gaze.

'Tell me one thing,' he breathed. 'Were you. . . ? Was you. . . ?'

'You didn't take a bullet defending no outlaw if that's what you're asking.'

A faint smile played on John's lips.

'What did you do?'

'I killed a man, but I did it to save other innocent people, a bit like you just did.'

13

John nodded. He opened his mouth to say something else, but the words were low and unintelligible.

For several more minutes Dalton sat with him, keeping a silent vigil as his breathing slowed until it finally stopped. And then Dalton was alone with two dead men and before him was the freedom he never thought he'd enjoy again.

He stood, pondering how best to use that freedom, but then saw movement nearby. He flinched round until his gaze alighted on the other side of the river.

Edging out into the water was the first wagon in a sprawling line of wagons – the very people John Stanton had been waiting to meet.

And they would reach him in a matter of minutes.

CHAPTER 2

Dalton shrugged inside his new and slightly baggy clothes, then stood back from the two mounds of earth and stones he'd hastily scraped over the bodies of John Stanton and Deputy Vaughn. He had been practical and swapped his torn and battered clothing for John's clothes, then claimed his belongings, but he had dignified his saviour's memory by burying him.

He also reckoned that the people in the wagons would have noticed him, even if they hadn't seen what he had been doing. So, if he ran with the bodies unburied, they would reach the obvious conclusion that he'd murdered them. Now, he just had to acknowledge the wagon train, wait until it had passed, then head off to enjoy his freedom.

He mounted John's horse and nudged it forward to stand on the edge of the water.

The driver of the lead wagon, a grey-haired and wiry man, had almost waded through the river. He was carefully picking a route, checking that there weren't any channels or dangerous currents. Five other wagons had lined up on the edge of the water, the people noting his route. Eight other wagons had stopped further back and were corralling their livestock.

The lead man hailed Dalton, then headed his wagon

out on to dry land and pulled up beside him.

'You waiting for us?' he asked, leaning forward in his seat.

Dalton shrugged, unwilling to say too much as anything he said could require him to lie and so perhaps cast suspicion on his actions.

'Just enjoying the view.'

'I'm Virgil Wade.' Virgil's roving gaze passed over Vaughn's horse, which was now mooching by the side of the river, then moved on to consider the two graves. 'What happened here?'

As Dalton had had only limited time before the wagons reached him, the location behind a small mound was the most private place he could find for the graves and, in his haste, he'd forgotten about Vaughn's horse. Clearly, Virgil was the kind of man who missed nothing and Dalton saw no choice but to set off towards the mound, beckoning Virgil to follow him.

Virgil called over his shoulder for Jacob to take the reins. A younger man, who Dalton assumed was his son, climbed out of the wagon and into the seat to take the reins from him. Then Virgil jumped down to join Dalton, who led him from the trail.

They waded through the long grass until they reached the graves.

'Two men died in a gunfight,' Dalton said, bowing his head. 'I buried them.'

'Any idea who they were?'

Dalton was about to confirm that John Stanton was one of the men, but an idea came to him.

'Some papers they had on them showed that a deputy sheriff from Harmony called Vaughn was escorting a wanted man, Dalton, to Applegate. I reckon the prisoner

16

fought back and got the lawman's gun off him.'

'You could be wrong.' Virgil tipped back his hat and glanced around. 'Somebody could have bushwhacked them – like the Spitzer gang.'

'Perhaps you're right,' Dalton said, shrugging. 'There's plenty of danger out here for unwary travellers.'

Virgil gave a short nod, but he continued to glance around. Dalton watched him and from the nervous darting of his eyes, he decided that he was concerned because of his own fear of the dangers of the trail and not because he didn't believe Dalton's story.

Dalton relaxed as he joined Virgil in heading back to the wagon.

'It may sound selfish,' Virgil said, 'but at least John Stanton wasn't one of the dead men. We can't give you a description, but have you seen a man who looks likes he's waiting for us?'

Having planted the idea in Virgil's mind that a man called Dalton was dead, Dalton was already thinking about how he'd assume a new identity, but Virgil's comment about not knowing what John Stanton looked like set his mind racing. Instantly, he decided to try a bluff.

'Perhaps I didn't explain myself. I am John . . . John Stanton.'

'I read your letter,' Virgil said, narrowing his eyes. 'It made me think you'd be older.'

A letter had been amongst John's belongings and Dalton made a mental note to read it when he got the chance.

'Apologies for that.'

Virgil smiled and pointed at the line of wagons that were now fording the river.

'Then I'd be obliged if you'd help me get them across

the water.'

Even before Dalton could nod, Virgil shouted orders to the next wagon that would reach the riverside. And as that wagon emerged on to dry land, Dalton quickly thought through the implications of his bluff.

If he couldn't convince these settlers he was John Stanton, they were sure to reach the obvious conclusion that he'd murdered the two men. But if they did accept him, he could accompany them to their final destination, then begin a new life with a new identity.

Pleased with his sudden decision, Dalton made himself useful by lining the wagons up on dry land, then introduced himself to each group and repeated that everyone should avoid the long grass where he'd buried the bodies.

But it was only when the tenth wagon rolled onto dry land that Dalton learned that taking on a new identity would not be as simple as he'd hoped.

A young, red-haired man was sitting beside a woman. This man passed the reins to the woman then jumped down from his wagon and stood beside Dalton, peering at the distant mountains and shaking his head.

'Hard to believe there is a way over them,' he said.

'It sure is,' Dalton said, turning to join him in looking at the mountains.

The man patted Dalton's back. 'Then I sure am glad we hired the best damn guide around.'

Dalton nodded then directed the next wagon to head on by, but the wagon had stopped before the comment filtered through to his thoughts.

And then he couldn't help but wince.

These people reckoned *he* was their guide and they expected him to lead them to their final destination. And with mounting shock, he realized that to do that he would have to find a route over the mountains when he didn't know what was on the other side of those mountains, or on this side, or even what the name of the mountains was.

Dalton sat beside the camp-fire, enjoying his broth, but eating slowly to avoid anyone learning just how desperately hungry he was.

The first few hours spent under his new identity had gone smoothly.

By late afternoon the wagons had safely crossed the river after which the group had said prayers over the graves of Deputy Vaughn and John Stanton and erected simple crosses labelled Vaughn and Dalton.

Then Virgil had insisted that they cover a few more miles that day, but everyone else reckoned that spending time fishing to replenish their provisions would be more useful. Virgil had still urged them to carry on but a round of grumbling from everyone persuaded him that they should settle down for the night.

While they settled, Dalton had distanced himself from the group, avoiding anyone drawing him into conversation in which he might have to tell more lies. He used the moments when nobody was looking his way to rummage through John's belongings and search for a map. But he didn't find one and, aside from the letter, neither did he uncover any more details about the man whose identity he had assumed.

And the letter provided little help. It had an illegible signature and was a short message agreeing to his terms for the mission and offering a payment of one hundred dollars.

Luckily, nobody looked at him in an odd way as he went about his business and Dalton slowly relaxed as he accepted that the settlers had never met John Stanton before.

And so as he spooned the meal into his mouth, he planned his future actions.

He hadn't lied to John as his saviour lay dying. His crime had not deserved Deputy Vaughn's relentless pursuit, capture and brutal treatment. Nine months ago in the town of Harmony, Dalton had killed a worthless and corrupt man to save innocent lives, but as that worthless man was a lawman, he had faced the noose.

Now, the Dalton who had faced those charges was dead and buried and a new Dalton had a chance for something he had only dreamed of before – a fresh start amongst people who wouldn't prejudge him as being an outlaw.

But he could only enjoy that fresh start if he became the man this group wanted him to be.

When Dalton had eaten his broth, he took his bowl down to the river to wash it, then sat on a boulder on the edge of the water, contemplating. From here he could see the dark and jagged outline of the mountains against the night sky and he reckoned that at the undoubtedly slow speed this wagon train would travel, they were several days away, perhaps weeks.

And that would give him time to search for a route he could lead them on. That route would prove to be a difficult one with rivers and ravines to ford and forests to hack through, and dangers of a more human kind might confront them. But as the settlers expected to face hardship, they wouldn't know that better and safer routes were probably available. Provided Dalton found them a place where they could settle down, they should accept that he was who he claimed he was.

Feeling confident now with his situation, Dalton watched

everyone mill around, seeing in the group's quiet efficiency that they had been travelling together for some time.

But he noticed a man and woman standing apart from the group beside their wagon. They were watching him and talking, their closeness and low tones suggesting they were concerned.

And when Dalton searched his memory for a previous encounter with them, he recalled that the man was the one who had told him he would be their guide. He was Newell Boone and she was Eliza. He had assumed they were married. Although on noticing they both had red hair, he revised his assumption to their being siblings.

There was still a chance someone might have information about John Stanton and so might suspect he wasn't that man. So, rather than delay an inevitable problem, he beckoned them over with a short wave and a wide smile.

Newell and Eliza glanced at each other and she said something to Newell, which Dalton thought might have been her saying that there was nothing to worry about. Then they set off towards him.

Dalton stood. He kept his stance casual and his expression relaxed as Newell swung to a halt before him and raised a foot to place it flat against the boulder beside the river. Eliza stood beside him with her arms folded.

'I believe in plain speaking,' Newell said, leaning on his knee. 'So, why don't you see fit to talk to us?'

'I'm sorry,' Dalton said. 'I'm not ignoring you. I just haven't got round to spending time with everyone.'

'I understand that, but after the letters Father wrote to you, I thought you'd at least want to speak to Father.'

'I thought Virgil Wade wrote to me,' Dalton said, then

regretted offering such a lame comment.

Newell narrowed his eyes. 'Henry Boone wrote to you. What makes you think it was Virgil?'

Dalton shrugged. 'He's your leader.'

Newell snorted and glanced at Eliza, who echoed his snort.

'He likes to think he's leading us,' she said.

'Yeah,' Newell said, 'but this wagon train is Father's. It's just that he ain't well enough to lead us right now.'

'Newell,' Eliza said, placing a hand on his arm, 'he won't ever lead us again. Accept that, please.'

Newell glanced at her and although his back remained rigid and his expression firm-jawed, when he spoke his tone was soft.

'I won't accept that and neither will Father, and until he says otherwise, he is still our leader.' Newell swung round to face Dalton. 'But I want to know why John thinks Virgil wrote to him.'

Dalton glanced away, desperately sifting through various excuses. His cheeks warmed as he failed to think of a lie that would resolve the even bigger lie he'd told. But Eliza resolved his problem for him.

'You've embarrassed him,' she said. 'Just because you know lettering, it doesn't mean everyone does.'

Newell winced, colour rising in his cheeks, and Dalton provided a bashful smile.

'Sorry. I got me some learning. I was reading the letter earlier – you might have seen me. I can make out some words, but not all of them.' Dalton shrugged and rocked from foot to foot. 'To be honest, I got someone to read to me and then write back, but perhaps I didn't hear or remember all the details.'

Newell closed his eyes, breathing deeply, then opened them.

'I'm the one who should apologize. I didn't think. I guess from your viewpoint, Virgil looks as if he's our leader.'

Dalton nodded then leaned forward and lowered his voice.

'And he sure didn't volunteer the information that he didn't write to me or that he wasn't in charge.'

'*He* wouldn't.' Newell stepped aside, letting Eliza take Dalton's arm and lead him to the wagon.

'You can see Father now,' she said, 'but keep the visit short. He's dying—'

'He's ill,' Newell snapped, hurrying past them to stand before the wagon.

'He is *dying*,' Eliza said as she stopped. She released Dalton's arm to place both hands on her hips. 'He's got a week, perhaps more, perhaps less, but he's dying.'

Newell opened his mouth, his jaw rippling with the words he wanted to snap back, but then he slapped a fist against his thigh and swirled round.

'Just wait here and I'll check he's still able to see you.'

Newell climbed into the wagon, leaving Dalton facing Eliza.

'Don't be hard on him,' Dalton said. 'It's hard for some people to accept things like that.'

She flashed a smile. 'You're a kind and perceptive man. My brother is, too, but perhaps too kind sometimes.'

Dalton could think of nothing else to say or ask that wouldn't risk adding to the lies he'd already told these decent people. And for the first time he felt a twinge of shame for what he'd done. Unable to face Eliza's pleasant smile and trusting eyes, he looked away towards the distant mountains.

Presently, Newell emerged and signified that he could see Henry, so Dalton jumped on to the wagon.

Inside, Henry Boone lay beneath a blanket in a clear area amongst the family's stored furniture, his wizened form providing the slightest of bumps. His face was gaunt and sallow, but the deep-set eyes held the determination and intelligence of a man who should be leading this wagon train.

Unfortunately, the stench in the wagon confirmed that Eliza was right. It reeked of death. Sweet, cloying, permeating every scrap of cloth and piece of stored furniture, the reek was impossible to ignore, a smell that said this man was close to the end.

A bony and liver-spotted hand slipped out from beneath the blanket and beckoned Dalton to come closer.

Hunched over and breathing through his mouth, Dalton approached him and sat cross-legged beside his bed.

'Listen,' Henry said. His voice was deeper and more assured than Dalton had expected, but he still expelled a wave of rank air that curdled Dalton's stomach. 'Newell can't accept I don't have much longer, but I will die soon and before I die, I want to see where my people will settle down.'

Henry displayed an arc of blackened teeth, the fragile smile appearing to acknowledge that he was unlikely to get his wish, then he waved towards a chest at his side.

Dalton moved to open it, but when Henry grunted and gestured again, he collected the folded blanket that rested on the top. He brought it to Henry, who opened it, his tense jaw, intense gaze and shaking hands confirming that this simple action required all his failing strength and concentration to complete. When the blanket fell away, a simple wooden sign lay on his hands, and Henry swung it round to face Dalton.

'Sweet Valley,' Dalton read aloud. 'The name of the new settlement?'

'A fine name for a fine town.' Henry busied himself with folding the blanket over the sign, but his hands shook so badly the sign slipped. Dalton rescued it, receiving a murmured thanks. 'And how long will it take you to lead my people to a place worthy of this sign?'

Dalton placed the sign and blanket back on the chest, heaving a sigh of relief, as Sweet Valley wasn't a specific location, but a dying man's dream of an ideal place to live.

'Five days, maybe a week.'

A snorting cackle emerged from Henry's lips.

'Honest men make bad liars. Don't tell me what I want to hear. Tell me the truth.'

Faced with Henry's unquestioning acceptance of his role, Dalton found that no matter how much trouble it might make for him, he couldn't lie to a dying man.

He laid a hand on his bony shoulder. 'No matter what I have to do, you'll see Sweet Valley I promise.'

Henry stared into Dalton's eyes, then nodded.

'I know what that promise means and I accept it. I reckon that from on high, I will be able to see Sweet Valley, and even if I die on the way down, I'll have seen it.' Henry stared hard at Dalton, his gaze boring into him, but Dalton could find nothing to say in reply. 'So, when you see the valley for the first time, take me out of this wagon and show it to me. That's all I ask.'

Henry closed his eyes, the gesture effectively ending

their meeting.

But Dalton still sat beside him for another few minutes, listening to his rasping breathing. Only when Henry delivered a low snore did he leave the wagon.

'How is he?' Eliza asked, drawing him away from the wagon.

Dalton glanced around, seeing that Newell had gone.

'Asleep.'

'Good. He does that a lot these days. Did you tell him the truth about how long it'll take to get over the mountains? Virgil reckons it'll take at least two weeks, and he can't last that long, never mind the time it'll take to get to somewhere where we can settle down.'

'I didn't lie, but I promised I'll do everything I can to get him there.' Dalton ventured a smile. 'Why did he even make this journey in that condition?'

'He never told us he was ill. I guess he must have been fighting to avoid showing it for a long time, but when we neared Applegate, he collapsed. Virgil bought him a potion from a snake-oil seller, but that made him worse. And since then, he's just become weaker with every passing day.'

Dalton tried to think of something comforting to say, but found that he couldn't face talking any more now that his bluff could hurt such decent people. He bade Eliza goodbye, then headed to the river, leaving her to slip into the wagon.

But when he'd settled down on the boulder by the river he looked towards the mound of earth that covered the body of the real John Stanton.

'I promise you, John,' he whispered under his breath, 'I won't let you down. I really won't. Whatever it takes and no matter if my bluff fails, I will get these settlers to Sweet Valley.'

CHAPTER 3

Dalton's first few days with the wagon train passed without any major problems.

Virgil didn't even consult him before they set off each day. Instead, he steered the wagons on a straight course across the plains towards the mountains, driving them on with a determination to cover as many miles as possible before the light dimmed.

Each day they closed on the mountains, but their forms grew so slowly that Dalton reckoned he still had several days before he had to trust his luck and choose a route.

But for now, nobody asked him for details of the terrain ahead, and neither did Dalton encourage that debate by letting himself get drawn into conversations where he'd be forced to lie or change the subject.

And his bluff weighed heavily on him. These people had every year of past hardship etched into their lined faces and work-calloused bodies. He didn't enquire into anyone's past, but assumed everybody had a reason for seeking out a new life in a new land. And the potential cost to them of trusting a man, who might not be able to find that new land, shamed Dalton into avoiding contact with them.

At night, the group did relax from the rigours of their journey. They placed the wagons in a circle with a heaped fire in the centre. The children milled and chased each other within the circle while the adults entertained themselves with simple pleasures such as swapping stories, singing, or playing games. In particular they enjoyed a game in which two competitors threw horseshoes at a spike in the ground. Jacob, Virgil Wade's son, was proficient at this game and usually emerged as champion.

Like Dalton, Eliza and Newell distanced themselves from the entertainment. If this was because their father was dying or because they were annoyed that Virgil had assumed control of the group, Dalton couldn't tell. But he didn't speak to them to find out, as he found it hard to talk to people who would suffer the most from his possible inability to direct them.

He did watch them, looking for signs of distress that might herald Henry's impending demise. He saw none and although Eliza assumed all the caring duties, many people passed by their wagon to offer help and to ask about Henry. From the snippets of conversation that Dalton overheard, he learned that his condition had even improved slightly.

On the fourth night, when he'd collected his meal, Eliza sat beside him. She said nothing other than to smile at him and they ate in silence, but afterwards, she took his plate and pointed to Henry's wagon.

'Father would like to talk to you again,' she said.

'What about?'

'He said it was a personal matter.' She leaned forward, a flash of intrigue in her lively eyes. 'I'll feed him later. You can see him first.'

Dalton still wavered, knowing that he would be unable to lie to Henry.

'He's a sick man. Are you sure I should bother him?'

'He knows his own mind, as he always has.' She placed a hand on his arm and squeezed. 'I know you're a quiet man who doesn't like to waste time on idle chatter, but Father likes that in a man. And I do, too.'

She ushered him away and, with her bemusing comment still on his thoughts, he headed into the wagon.

Henry was sitting up, with more colour in his cheeks than the last time he'd seen him.

'You look well,' Dalton said with all honesty.

'I *do* feel better. Odd that, but I like the nights now that it's getting colder.' Henry gestured to the flapping cloth at the back of the wagon. 'And that must mean we're making good progress.'

'We are. But this is the easy part. We'll travel more slowly later.' Dalton settled down beside Henry. 'But you had a personal matter you wanted to talk to me about.'

Henry chuckled, the sound rasping. 'I do have a personal concern that only a dying man with a comely daughter would raise. I reckon you're a man who likes plain speaking. So, you said in your letter that you'd thought of settling down one day. Are you still considering that?'

Dalton gulped as he instantly saw the direction this conversation was taking.

'I am,' he said, his tone cautious.

'And now that you've met Eliza, do you think you and she might. . . ?' Henry raised his eyebrows.

Dalton sighed. Until Eliza had uttered her cryptic comment before he'd come into the wagon, he hadn't thought about her at all. Now, he found to his surprise that the insinuation didn't disconcert him.

'It's hard to say.'

'I know I'm putting you in a difficult position. You don't want to lie to a dying man, but at least tell me you'll consider her. Jacob Wade is the only man here who could be suitable, and he ain't.'

Dalton shrugged. 'Aside from watching him play that game with the horseshoes, I haven't talked to him, but he seems a fine young man.'

Henry shivered. 'Ain't got the energy for the details, but the Wade family are no good, no good at all. And where we're going, Eliza won't meet many men. I'd hate to die without knowing one of my kin will give me grandchildren.'

Dalton considered Henry's wicked smile and he returned it.

'You're a fiendish old man and that's a fact.'

Henry cackled, the sound ending in a burst of coughing, but the merriment still played in his deep-set eyes.

'I like you, John. You won't lie and you won't give up. Do what you will and I'm sure Eliza will get her claws into you. Now, I'm hungry. Send her in.' Henry winked. 'But I won't keep her long if you want to talk to her later.'

Dalton patted Henry's shoulder then left the wagon.

Eliza was loitering nearby and she hurried over to join him.

'What did he want?' she asked, rising on her toes to peer over his shoulder at the wagon.

'Like you said, it was a personal matter.'

'And did you promise him he'd get to see Sweet Valley? He's been better these last few days and there has to be a chance.'

Dalton considered her hopeful expression and although supporting her suggestion would provide him with a ready explanation, he shook his head.

'That wasn't what he wanted to ask me.'

'Father tells me everything,' she said, her voice low and hurt as she hunched her shoulders and folded her arms.

Dalton placed a hand on her shoulder. 'It was nothing to worry about, and now he's hungry. That has to be another good sign.'

'It is.' She patted his hand, then rocked her head up to look at him and gave a wicked smile that proved she was her father's daughter. 'But if you won't tell me what he said, I'll have to see what I can get out of him.'

'Don't pester him,' Dalton said. He smiled. 'Perhaps we can . . . we can talk later after you've fed him.'

She nodded. 'I'd like that.'

He gestured through a gap in the circle of wagons.

'And maybe we could walk down to the creek. It looks like it'll be a fine night.'

Her eyes flashed before she looked away, breathing deeply, and Dalton thought he might have been too forward, that she'd refuse, but she smiled.

'That would be nice. So long as Newell approves.'

'Later, then.'

She turned to the wagon and Dalton was sure she gave a short skip, but then she halted. Her shoulders shook. Then she swirled round, her eyes blazing.

'That was the personal matter he talked to you about, wasn't it?'

'I . . . I . . .' Dalton stammered as she advanced on him.

She stabbed a finger against his chest, punctuating her points with repeated stabs.

31

'He told you I'm growing into a spinster woman, didn't he? He told you that where we're going there just aren't any men, didn't he? He told you that you should . . . should woo me, didn't he? Go on. Deny that.'

'I can't. But it wasn't like that. He just said that—'

She delivered a stinging slap to his cheek that resounded around the circle of wagons and, from the corner of his eye, Dalton saw several heads snap round to watch them with interest and amusement.

'You can forget whatever plans you and Father have dreamed up because I will not go walking down by the creek with the likes of you.'

She swirled round, her long skirt swinging, and flounced to the wagon.

While rubbing his cheek, Dalton watched her climb into the wagon, then immediately climb back out again to collect her father's meal, then disappear inside.

Dalton was aware that several people were still watching him and murmuring to each other with curiosity in their tones, but he ignored them and continued to watch the wagon.

Presently she emerged, but she saw that Dalton was watching the wagon and turned on her heel. She slipped away through the gap between Henry's wagon and the next one, muttering under her breath, then walked off into the night, heading down to the creek.

But just as she disappeared from view, she glanced back over her shoulder.

And then she was gone.

Dalton watched the darkness between the wagons for another minute, then shook himself.

'Dalton,' he said to himself as he headed after her,

'you're in serious trouble.'

When he was beyond the circle of wagons, he stopped and waited for his eyes to adjust to the dark.

The half-moon was low and providing some light, but deep shadows pooled on the ground. Dalton squinted and slowly Eliza's form resolved standing by the creek and looking into the water.

The creek was around ten feet wide and the water's gurgling as it brushed over rocks came to Dalton on a light and sweet breeze. He watched her bend and cup a handful of water, which she drew up to her face, but she didn't drink.

Slowly, she let the water drip down to the creek, the droplets small balls of fire in the moonlight, then she cupped another handful. She appeared so serene, her gestures almost suggestive of ritual. Dalton rocked from foot to foot, uncertain as to what he should do.

When he'd followed her he had been sure that she had wanted him to do just that, but now he was less sure. Had her last glance back been her way of requesting his company? Or had it meant something entirely different?

One thing was certain – a bad guess would have repercussions.

He watched her through another cycle of cupping water and letting it drip to the creek, then made his decision and set off. Whether she wanted to see him or not, he detected in himself an urge to see her and at the very least explain himself.

But he still paced carefully, placing his feet to the ground in the pools of inky blackness and avoiding startling her until he was closer and could call out to her.

When he'd walked to within twenty paces of the creek,

she straightened and threw the last handful of water over her shoulder. Her shoulders and arms shook, although as she had her back to him, he couldn't tell what she was doing.

But then she swirled round to look down the creek.

'Jacob,' she murmured, backing a pace, her tone startled, 'is that you again?'

Dalton opened his mouth, meaning to apologize, but the words died on his lips. He had not been the one to startle her. A man was standing, emerging from the shadows between two rocks.

'It ain't,' the man said, 'Eliza Boone.'

'Who . . . who are you? What do you want?'

'You know what we want.'

'We?' she bleated, then flinched. The first note of a scream tore from her lips but then died as another man emerged from behind her and slapped a hand over her mouth.

Both men must have been hiding in the shadows down by the creek, possibly waiting for her, and neither of the men was from the wagon train.

'You two,' Dalton shouted at the top of his voice, ensuring that they and anyone else who was nearby heard him, 'step away from Eliza.'

Dalton heard an instant commotion erupt from behind him and confident now that he'd alerted everyone to the danger, he broke into a run. He didn't have the gun he'd taken from John on him and could see that both men were packing guns, but he didn't slow as he closed on them.

The man holding Eliza from behind turned her round to face Dalton, and barked out a command that he stay back, but heartened by Dalton's presence, Eliza fought back. She stamped on the man's foot, elbowed him in the stomach, and squirmed and struggled in his grip.

The other man hurried along the creek to help him, his body turned towards Dalton, his gun drawn.

Dalton slid to a halt and raised his hands slightly.

'You won't get away with this. Help is a-coming. Put down that gun, release Eliza, and run while you still got the chance.'

The man darted his gaze up past Dalton, where Dalton could hear pounding footfalls as several men hurried out through the wagons and others shouted that Eliza was in danger.

He moved to join his associate in holding Eliza, but she bent at the waist and threw herself forward, the movement making her assailant slip on the wet ground beside the creek and they both came tumbling down.

Dalton broke into a run, hurtling across the ground towards them.

The standing man glanced up at him, then ran, splashing through the shallow water and away. Then Dalton reached the struggling twosome.

He slapped a hand on the man's back and dragged him away from Eliza to stand him straight, then delivered a round-armed slug to his jaw with all the pent-up anger of the last few minutes behind it.

The man reeled to the ground as Dalton grabbed Eliza's shoulders, lifted her from the ground and threw her in the general direction of the approaching help from the wagon train. Then he stood between her and the man, waiting for him to rise.

When the man came up, his hand reaching for his gun,

Dalton kicked his hand away. Then he thundered a blow into his cheek, wheeling him away into the creek where he landed on his back with his arms and legs splayed, a huge splash spraying water around him.

Dalton stomped down into the shallows, ready to capture him, but the man rolled backwards and this time, when he came up, he stood crouched in the water with his gun drawn.

Dalton immediately danced back, the man too far away for him to reach, then dived to the ground.

A gunshot ripped out. Dalton heard the whine as it scythed into the dirt, a few feet to his side. Dalton pressed himself flat to the earth, trusting that Eliza had had the sense to keep running, and that in the poor light the man wouldn't be able to see either of them from the creek.

A second shot peeled out. Dalton winced, but then realized the report had come from behind him, a fact confirmed when he saw the man roll out of the creek on the other side and run off in the direction the other man had fled.

Dalton still stayed down, ensuring that the man wouldn't hit him with a wild shot, but the man didn't fire again and by the time a surge of people joined Dalton, both men had disappeared into the gloom.

Several men were keen to chase after them, but Virgil called for order. Everyone still continued to murmur, but sufficient quiet returned for Dalton to hear the clop of hoofs as the men secured the horses they must have left nearby.

After a short discussion everyone agreed that there was little chance of chasing after and securing the raiders in the night. Several people reckoned these men were with the Spitzer gang, a group of bandits they had been warned about in Applegate and who terrorized the area and specifically preyed on travellers.

'Is Eliza all right?' Dalton asked, when everyone turned to head back to the wagons.

'She is,' Virgil said, 'and that's entirely down to you.'

The group raised a clamour of support for Dalton's actions and, embarrassed by the congratulations, he wended his way through a crowd of backslapping men until he reached Newell, who was standing outside Henry's wagon.

'What did they want?' Newell asked, his eyes wide and staring, his demeanour more shocked than pleased.

'Eliza, apparently. They knew her by name.'

Newell winced. 'Why did they know that? Why did they know that?'

Dalton reckoned he wasn't expecting an answer, and he patted his back and headed past him. But standing on the other side of the wagon was Eliza and, like Newell, she didn't look pleased, her eyes were blazing and her actions jerky as she brushed dust from her skirt.

'That must have been a terrible shock,' Dalton said.

'It was,' she said through clenched teeth.

'Did you recognize them?'

'No.'

Dalton accepted that she didn't want to talk about her ordeal and he moved to pass by her, but she raised a hand, halting him.

'But I *did* recognize you.'

Dalton smiled. 'I'm just glad I was there and could help.'

'I didn't mean that. I mean why were you there in the

first place? I went down to the creek to bathe and you followed me. You . . . You . . . You disgust me. I thought you were different from the likes of Jacob Wade, but you're just as pathetic as he is. Never ever do that to me again.'

Dalton flinched back, shrugging. 'I'm sorry. I thought. . . .'

He turned and headed away, sighing and shaking his head.

'And John,' she called after him. 'Thank you. I'm glad you did follow me.'

Dalton stopped to nod, then headed away.

While the wagon train prepared to move out on Dalton's fifth day with the group, Dalton avoided Eliza. Although Newell did look at him and give a rueful smile, as if acknowledging that he was embarrassed at not being more grateful the previous night.

All the settlers were tense; the encounter with the Spitzer gang had subdued everyone. For the first time since Dalton had joined the wagon train they had maintained a permanent watch through the night. The gang hadn't returned and when the wagons moved on outlying riders scouted around, ensuring they got advance warning of any more raids by these notorious bandits.

Despite this, the wagons made good speed, everyone appearing eager to get to their new life where they hoped they wouldn't have to deal with such problems.

And last night's incident soon left Dalton's immediate thoughts as his first big decision crept up on him.

So far, he hadn't needed to advise Virgil as to the direction they should take. The wagon train had just headed across the plains towards the mountains, but now the land was rising.

Ahead, the deep indentations of gorges and ridges were slowly revealing themselves and their foreboding presence confirmed that if he chose the wrong route, he could lead them into an impassable dead end.

He continually peered ahead, running his gaze over the various potential routes and hoping he would see which one would give him them the best chance of success. But all routes appeared equally treacherous and Dalton slowly accepted the truth of his dilemma. Henry Boone wouldn't have hired a guide in advance if the route ahead was an obvious one and for him to lead them to Sweet Valley would require a huge slice of luck.

As the day wore on, the moment when he needed to discover just how lucky he would be arrived. A river, perhaps the same one as the one where he'd met the wagons, was lazily swinging in to block their path and he had to choose between fording it or heading upriver.

Dalton darted his gaze around as he searched for which alternative would be the better.

And it was then that he had the stroke of luck he'd hoped for.

A rider was arcing in towards the wagon train from the river and had a hand held high as he hailed them. Since Dalton had joined the group, this was the first traveller they'd encountered during the day.

Virgil shouted orders down the line of wagons for every one to be on their guard, but Dalton judged that this man wouldn't give the same sort of trouble as the Spitzer gang had. He hurried his horse on to speak to him privately and perhaps glean information about what was ahead.

'Howdy,' he called. 'You heading in any particular direction?'

The man introduced himself as Loren Steele, then pointed to the mountains.

'Going that-a-way.'

Dalton kept his face impassive, avoiding reacting to this good news.

'That's where we're heading. You been over them before?'

'Nope.' Loren leaned forward in the saddle, smiling. 'But it sure is good news that we're heading to the same place. Be obliged if you'd let me join you.'

Dalton bit back his disappointment, then glanced back to see that Virgil Wade was speeding his wagon to join them, with riders flanking him and glaring at Loren.

'Ain't really my place to say.'

Loren rocked his gaze from Dalton to the advancing Virgil, then nodded and stayed quiet until Virgil joined them. Then he made his pitch.

'I ain't no trouble,' he said. 'I ain't no burden. I can help with anything and ask for nothing in return, and I got no needs other than to enjoy good company.'

Virgil didn't reply immediately, sizing Loren up with his steady gaze, then he looked around, perhaps to see if this man had any associates. He glanced at Dalton.

Dalton had caught only fleeting glimpses of the Spitzer gang in the dark, but he was sure he would recognize them if he met them in daylight. And he saw nothing in Loren's placid gaze and honest expression to alarm him. He nodded to Virgil, who returned the nod then pointed towards the wagons, signifying that Loren could ride along with them. Then he turned to Dalton.

'Do we cross the river?' he asked.

Dalton took a deep breath and entrusted his first guess to luck. Loren had been riding away from the river and, as his horse's flanks were wet, he must have forded it. So, that suggested there wasn't an obvious route on the other side of the river.

He pointed upriver. Without further word, Virgil headed his wagon off along the side of the river.

Dalton watched the wagon pass by, then turned to follow, but Loren hadn't moved and was still watching him.

'So,' he said, 'you're guiding these people, are you?'

'Sure am,' Dalton said. 'I'm John Stanton.'

Loren's gaze remained expressionless as he gave a slow nod.

'Well met, John . . . Stanton.'

Dalton caught an odd intonation in the way Loren uttered the name and the slow way he'd used the full name was also odd.

He dismissed that from his mind and turned to follow Virgil, but as he rode off, he had the distinct impression that Loren was watching his back.

The steadily rising trail that Dalton had chosen presented no problems that day and neither did anyone catch sight of the Spitzer gang. So, when they made camp that night, Dalton was in good spirits, and those good spirits had infused the rest of the group.

He studiously avoided Eliza and the only time their paths crossed was when Dalton slipped out of the circle of wagons to collect water from the river. She happened to be standing in his way, but she turned and started talking with the guard assigned to keep an eye on anyone leaving the circle.

After that, Dalton did what he normally did in the evenings and sat apart from the group, watching everyone and enjoying the sight of their relaxed camaraderie.

As darkness fell, Virgil posted another two men outside the circle to watch out for the bandits and issued orders that nobody should leave the circle unaccompanied. But within the circle, the group built up the fire, raised their voices and laughed loudly at any comment.

Dalton quickly saw that this wasn't because everybody had forgotten the near tragic events of last night, but was in direct defiance of those events. If the Spitzer gang were close, everybody was letting them know that they weren't frightened and that they would prevail.

In spite of his earlier apparent suspicion, Loren didn't look at him again, although Dalton had the impression that he was avoiding looking at him. But Dalton accepted that if he were paranoid about every encounter he would never survive this journey. He dismissed his worries from his mind so that he could enjoy watching everyone have fun.

The game of throwing horseshoes at a spike started up and tonight Jacob Wade was even more impressive than normal, winning every match and eventually taking on all comers and defeating them. The game was over seven shoes and Jacob lost only one or at most two rounds before winning each game.

As the night wore on Jacob was indefatigable, his face beaming and the air frequently receiving a firm punch as he won yet again. The only time he moved away from the spike was to receive the congratulations of the watching people. Dalton couldn't help but notice that he always talked to someone close to wherever Eliza happened to be sitting and often glanced in her direction.

But he didn't speak to her and neither did she look at him while he was close.

Dalton had never played a game of this kind before and so had no desire to participate. But after Jacob had won his twentieth straight game by defeating Loren Steele with four perfect throws, Jacob boasted that nobody would ever beat him again.

His boast received catcalls aplenty, but nobody stepped forward to challenge that claim and Dalton surprised himself as much as anyone when he found himself rising to his feet and pacing into the circle of watchers to stand before him.

'You can't say you can defeat anyone,' he said, 'because you haven't played me yet.'

Dalton glanced around the watching circle, seeing both Eliza and Loren lean forward with interest, and hearing everyone else welcome him with a huge cheer. He acknowledged the encouragement with a short wave, then returned his gaze to the beaming Jacob.

'Then,' Jacob said, rolling his shoulders, 'it's time to find out if you're a good loser.'

CHAPTER 4

Dalton reckoned he'd set himself up for a quick defeat, but he got plenty of encouragement from a group eager to see the boastful Jacob defeated by a man who had already proved his worth. And he milked the situation, pacing around behind the mark, sizing up the spike from various angles, crouching down then standing as he chose the best angle from which to throw.

He'd watched the others throw and noted that many threw the shoe high in the air, aiming to land it on the spike, but Jacob threw hard and low, trusting his accurate aim to catch the spike and hang on. He decided to use Jacob's tactic.

His first throw worked perfectly, slamming into the spike then spinning around it and coming to rest with the spike in the centre of the shoe.

A huge cheer rippled around the circle of watchers as Jacob grumbled about the throw being a lucky one, then took his place behind the mark. And perhaps Dalton's unexpected success had rattled him because his shoe flew a foot or so over the spike, giving Dalton the lead.

Spurred on by the success of his first throw, Dalton tried the same tactic for his next two throws, but he missed the spike both times and, with Jacob catching his shoe around the spike, he lost both rounds.

After that, he threw his fourth shoe with more care and less strength and it landed in the dirt in front of the spike, then slid across the earth to nudge up to the spike. In response, Jacob delivered an accurate throw, but it hit the spike and ricocheted, landing further away than Dalton's throw.

The loser always took the first throw of the next round and, with the game tied and with only three throws remaining, Dalton appraised his opponent.

Jacob strode back and forth considering the spike from a variety of angles and repeatedly rocking his arm up and down as he tested the weight before throwing.

Eventually he threw, but even after all his preparation, the shoe emerged from his hand with too low a trajectory and ploughed into the dirt four feet short of the spike, then stopped dead.

Jacob muttered an oath under his breath, kicked at the dirt, then swung round and stomped past Dalton.

'Bad luck,' Dalton said.

'I'll get you next time,' Jacob grunted.

Dalton smiled as he considered Jacob's hunched shoulders and downcast eyes.

'There's nothing at stake here,' he said, still smiling. 'Don't take it so seriously.'

Jacob snapped his head up to glower at Dalton, his glaring eyes confirming that he took all competitive situations seriously. Dalton shook his head as he turned away, but he did wave to the watchers, encouraging everyone to support him.

Somehow, he'd rattled his opponent more than anyone

else had tonight and the watchers did their best to strengthen Dalton's position, clapping and shouting encouragement. And as he took up his position, he noticed Jacob look around. His gaze centred on Eliza, who was talking animatedly with Newell.

Dalton nodded to himself, reckoning that he had understood the situation and the reason why he had been the one who had rattled Jacob. Confident now of his ability to beat him, he cleared his mind of all distracting thoughts and concentrated on beating Jacob's poor throw.

He centred his gaze on the spike as he weighed the shoe in his hand then threw it, but as it left his hand, a light flashed in his eyes, dazzling him and making him flinch. The shoe flew wildly away, landing ten feet to the side and five feet beyond the spike.

A collective sigh went up from the watchers as Dalton straightened then looked around for what had dazzled him. And Jacob was thrusting his hand beneath his jacket while sporting a smug grin.

Dalton stared at him as Jacob held his hand out, inviting him to take the next throw.

Dalton collected both shoes then paced to the side to keep his back to Jacob and threw the shoe using his previous tactic of aiming strongly at the spike. The shoe clanged into the spike and although it didn't catch, it dropped to the dirt a few inches from the spike, leaving Jacob in the position of needing an accurate throw to win the game.

Jacob took up his position behind the mark, walking slowly by Dalton.

'Reckon as I'll beat you this time,' he said, swinging his arms and grinning.

'If you have to cheat to win, you're welcome to it.'

'No such thing as cheating in this game.' Jacob crouched, then rocked his hand back and forth. 'All that matters is to win.'

'And does that apply to everything?' Dalton glanced over Jacob's shoulder to look in Eliza's general direction.

Jacob straightened then turned to look at Eliza. He turned back, his smug grin re-emerging.

'Yeah. I'll beat you at everything, old man.'

Dalton nodded. 'I reckon I understand. But what I don't understand is why you reckon that beating me at this childish game will impress a woman like Eliza.'

Jacob resumed his crouched stance and rocked back his hand, ready to throw.

'This is just a part of it.'

'For you, it's the *only* part.' Dalton waited for Jacob to swing his hand forward before delivering his final comment. 'You can have this game, I'll have Eliza.'

Jacob flinched as he threw, Dalton's taunt causing his aim to veer, and the shoe flew over the top of the spike to land five feet on, then roll onwards for several more feet. Jacob swirled round to glare at him.

'I thought you didn't believe in cheating.'

'I never said that. I can beat you any way I choose, kid.' Dalton held out his hand. 'And now it's your throw again – one each for the game.'

Jacob grumbled as he collected both shoes. He threw one to Dalton's feet then rolled his shoulders and took up his position.

'You forget, old man,' he muttered while staring at the spike. 'I'm Eliza's age, I know her better than you do, and I'm staying. I'll beat you to her just like I'll beat you at this game.'

Jacob glanced at Dalton, his eye flared, then he turned

to look at the spike and threw the shoe.

If it hadn't been for Jacob's arrogance, Dalton would have been impressed as the shoe flew at the spike, hit it, then slid into place around the spike to sit nudging up to it – a perfect throw and unbeatable.

Jacob slapped his hands together then straightened and walked past Dalton without further comment, letting his good throw say everything he needed to say.

Dalton hefted his shoe and considered how he could match Jacob's throw, finding in himself a surprising yearning to succeed. A few minutes ago he had had no interest in even playing this game, and he didn't share Jacob's desire to show off in front of Eliza.

But now the competitive urge had taken him over and he had to find a way to beat Jacob.

He pulled his hat low in case Jacob tried to dazzle him again then stared at the spike as he rocked his arm back and forth. He couldn't beat Jacob's throw, but as the bluff he'd been carrying out since he'd joined the settlers required him to ride his luck, he decided to trust that luck again and use the same tactic as for his first throw.

He thrust his arm back, then hurled the shoe at the spike with all his strength. The shoe blurred through the air, then cracked into the tip of the spike. It caught, then swirled round and round. Applause and cheering broke out, but Dalton still stared at the spinning shoe, the strength he'd used letting it spin for many seconds.

But the shoe didn't come loose and nestled down on top of Jacob's shoe.

'A tie,' Virgil Wade declared, coming into circle with his arms held wide. 'A fair result after the best game of the night.'

'We got to throw again,' Jacob shouted, slapping his

hands on his hips and pouting, 'and prove who's the best. And that's me.'

Virgil looked at Dalton, but Dalton reckoned he'd pushed his luck far enough with his last throw and shook his head.

'A tie is a fair result for me.'

Jacob grumbled and even stamped a foot. Then the three men stood in a silent group, each man glancing at the others. Dalton could see from Virgil's gleaming eyes and proud smile that he approved of his son's competitive spirit, but that only helped to convince Dalton he didn't want to continue with the game.

He started to confirm that as far as he was concerned the game had ended with honours even, when Newell Boone emerged from the circle to stand over the spike. He stared down at it, rocking his head from side to side, then beckoned them to join him.

'We don't need another game to see who's won,' he said. 'We already know. John's shoe is the nearest to the spike.'

'What?' Virgil and Jacob snapped together as they hurried over to join Newell.

Dalton followed and saw that Newell was right. Jacob's shoe had been touching the spike, but Dalton's throw had been so powerful it had pushed the shoe away to leave his being the only one touching the spike. The gap was only an inch, but it was still there.

'See,' Newell said. 'John won the game.'

'Jacob's shoe was touching the spike,' Virgil said. 'The best John could do was to tie. He couldn't win.'

'He could,' Newell declared, miming the action of Dalton's shoe hitting the spike and pushing Jacob's away with his hands, 'but only if he knocked Jacob's shoe away, and that's just what he's done.'

'*That* is not the rules of the game.'

'It is. The nearest shoe wins.'

'Not when the first thrower touches the spike.'

Newell sneered. 'You just made that rule up.'

Dalton watched the two men knock this argument back and forth, waiting for an opportunity to butt in and state that he didn't mind settling for a tie, but he saw that Virgil and Newell weren't arguing about this game. A simpler power-struggle was coming out into the open – perhaps for the first time – and one in which neither man was prepared to back down.

But one of them had to relent and, as the circle of watchers broke up in disgust at their pointless argument, Virgil's position of arguing that the nearest shoe shouldn't win started to sound desperate.

And to Dalton's surprise, Virgil suddenly backed away.

'All right,' he said, waving a hand in a dismissive manner as he turned his back on Newell, 'if this means that much to you, I'll declare that John has won.'

'That's only because he did,' Newell said, folding his arms.

'He didn't,' Jacob muttered, advancing on Newell. 'You cheating Boones can't deny me.'

Newell glanced at Jacob, shook his head then turned away, but Jacob broke into a run, thrust his head down, and slammed into Newell's side. The sudden nature of his action caught Newell unawares and he wheeled his arms and legs as he fought to keep his balance, but Jacob carried him on. The two men tumbled to the ground.

Within seconds, both men were rolling over each other, throwing dust up as they tried to land flailing blows on the other man. Wild scything punches connected on arms and shoulders, but from so close neither man could inflict much damage on the other.

The watchers stood bemused and rigid, Dalton getting the impression that even if they were on guard to repel the Spitzer gang, violence amongst their own numbers was rare. And it was only when Eliza fought her way through the circle of watchers and tried to get a restraining hand on Newell's back that everyone broke out of their spell.

Dalton and Virgil hurried towards the fighters. Newell had now pinned Jacob on his back and was shaking his shoulders, knocking his head back into the dirt.

Virgil reached them first. He nudged Eliza aside, then looped his hands under Newell's armpits and lifted him off Jacob, who used his freedom to throw a wild punch at Newell. His fist whistled through the air a foot short of Newell's chin. Then he rolled to his feet and hurled back his fist ready to aim another punch at him, but Dalton grabbed Jacob around the chest from behind.

Newell and Jacob squirmed and struggled, trying to wrestle themselves clear and land a punch or a kick on the other man, but when Virgil and Dalton dragged them apart, they slowly desisted.

Dalton heard Virgil murmur placating words to Newell, and Eliza joined them, shaking her head.

'Let me go,' Jacob whined.

'I will,' Dalton said, keeping his voice low as he spoke into Jacob's ear, 'but only when you're not so loco.'

'You don't know what this is about.'

'I got an idea and I'll give you a good piece of advice – beating on Eliza's brother sure ain't the right way to impress her.'

Jacob snorted. 'That ain't got nothing to do with why I hate the Boone family. They don't lead this group. We do.'

'We both know you don't hate *all* the Boone family.' Dalton relaxed his hold of Jacob's chest to give him more leeway. 'I know this is hard for you, but you got to be sensible.'

'Leave me alone. I don't need your pity.'

Dalton detected a change in Jacob's tone, with hurt feelings replacing his anger, and he released his grip to let him stand free.

'Then take a different piece of advice. No matter whose fault this is, you all have to live together. Shake Newell's hand.'

Jacob rolled his shoulders. 'I'll never do that.'

'Then do it for Eliza.' Dalton moved from behind Jacob to stand before him. 'Or you'll stand no chance against me.'

Jacob sneered. 'I already have everything I need to impress her. You'll see.'

Jacob brushed by him and paced towards Newell, who glared at him, but then swung away and left the circle of wagons. A few moments later another man returned, confirming that Jacob had taken over his guard duties.

With the cause of the fight having left, Virgil released Newell and headed off after his son.

Everyone else dispersed, disappearing into their wagons with barely a word or glance at each other, and neither Eliza nor Newell looked at Dalton as they headed to Henry's wagon.

With the area clearing in a matter of minutes, Dalton turned on the spot to find that only one person remained – Loren Steele.

'Now,' Loren said, smiling as he glanced in the direction Jacob and Virgil had gone, 'you dealt with that situation well, John Stanton.'

Then Loren tipped his hat and turned away.

In the morning nobody mentioned last night's incident, although from the significant glances he detected being exchanged, Dalton judged that most people were embarrassed but not surprised by the confrontation.

He also noticed that more people than usual called in on Henry Boone's wagon to check that he had had a restful night.

When they were ready to move out, in accordance with the normal routine, Virgil took up the lead position and, with a few terse questions, requested instructions on their route today. As Dalton hoped that the river would have flowed from the higher ground down a route they could follow, he directed him to continue following the winding path of the river, keeping to its side.

For most of the morning they travelled at a steady rate. When the sun had burnt off the early mist Dalton saw that the river was now flowing down a valley, its sides becoming increasingly steep. And they were closing on a range of jagged peaks and rocky ridges. But Dalton continued to hope that when they reached them the terrain would resolve itself into something less formidable than it appeared to be from further away.

For the whole morning this possibility remained. The steep-sided valley, and occasionally the thick forest, closed in so that there was room for only one wagon to pass easily beside the river.

But later the flat and gently rising land on either side of the river provided easy travelling, with the steep valley-sides and thick forest staying several hundred yards back. And on several occasions the sides of the valley became shallow enough to provide a passable way out of the valley if the route ahead were to became blocked.

As the day wore on those occasions became less frequent and the times when the land narrowed became more frequent.

Dalton began to feel that disaster would be around the next bend in the river. So, as they rounded each bend, he ensured he was at the front so that he'd be the first to see what was ahead. Each time, he hoped his luck would hold and that a path which this group could follow would be ahead.

But the valley continued to narrow and, just as the valley sides loomed on either side and he was fighting down his mounting panic, he rounded another bend.

Ahead, the valley straightened and a long and steep ascent caused the river to roar and spray over the rocky bed, and that ascent led to a solid ridge, with the land beyond disappearing from view.

Dalton couldn't help but let his gaze linger on the summit of that ascent, noting that beyond nothing was visible other than the clear blue sky. Even the jagged peaks were invisible behind this significant ridge.

He hoped that his luck would hold and that once they'd crested the ridge, there would be a negotiable continuation of their route. But he gave no sign of his concern as he shouted encouragement to everyone to follow and the wagons headed up the incline in single file.

Dalton centred his gaze on the blue sky, hoping he would soon see an indication that the terrain would be passable beyond the ridge.

But he got the first inkling that his luck was about to run out when he was half-way up the slope. He caught the first glimpse of the peak of a bluff that poked out from beyond the ridge, pines sprouting up from its top like unruly hair.

And as he closed on the crest of the ridge that bluff spread out to cover the whole of the route ahead.

Dalton fought back the growing feeling of despondency that threatened to overwhelm him. He speeded up to ensure he was well ahead of the group and so give himself time to decide where they would go next.

But when he crested the top, he could see no possible forward route.

He drew his horse to a halt and peered up the winding extent of the river, but it disappeared into a precipitous gorge. Both sides of the gorge were too steep for a rider to climb and perhaps even a man.

Dalton locked his gaze to the bluff that blocked their way on this side of the river, but the sides were vertical and even overhanging in places. And the slope on the other side of the river was rocky and ended in an overhang at the top.

There just wasn't any way forward from this position.

'Which route do we take now?' Virgil shouted from behind him as his wagon crested the ridge.

Dalton drew his horse back, still glancing around in the forlorn hope that he might find a path, but seeing no way out. Virgil drew his wagon to a halt and Dalton glanced at him, seeing his features reddening by the moment.

But it was Jacob who poked his head out from the wagon and delivered the simplest assessment of their situation.

'You've led us in the wrong direction,' he said, a certain smugness in his tone. 'What kind of guide are you?'

CHAPTER 5

Dalton forced himself to ignore Virgil's and Jacob's agitated complaints and peered around, searching for a possible way out of the dead end he'd led them into.

But he could see no route ahead and could think of nothing to say that would avoid him losing the settlers' confidence. The only possibility was for them to double back and for him to search for another route upwards.

'Well?' Virgil asked, his tone determined and demanding an answer. 'What are we going to do?'

Dalton turned and watched the next wagon crest the ridge, then raised his eyes to look down the snaking line of wagons trailing further down the slope.

Beyond the last wagon, movement caught his eye. He took a deep breath and turned in the saddle to look at Virgil.

'Keep your voice down,' he said, 'and look as if we're unconcerned, but move everyone over the ridge and seek the higher ground beside the gorge.'

Dalton pointed to the highest point the wagons would be able to reach below the most precipitous part of the gorge.

'Why?' Virgil asked, his eyes narrowing with suspicion.

'Because we're being followed and we need to prepare for the worst.'

Virgil gulped. 'You . . . You sure? Is it the Spitzer gang?'

Dalton couldn't help but notice the stammer in Virgil's voice.

'Don't know who they are, but they're staying back and for me, that means trouble. But don't worry. I've taken us to the best place to defend ourselves and we will prevail.'

Virgil hunched forward in his seat, then gave a quick nod and turned to pass an order down the line of wagons for everyone to move up over the ridge and make camp at the highest point they could reach. The driver of the next wagon looked at the impassable terrain ahead, but as Virgil had used a stern voice that left no room for debate, he followed his instructions.

As the wagons rattled past Virgil muttered further orders. From several of the wagons men jumped down then hurried along the line of wagons with rifles in hand and keeping out of the view of anyone who was further down the slope. They moved so swiftly that Dalton noted that this group must have a prearranged routine for dealing with trouble when on the move.

Loren crested the ridge between the sixth and seventh wagons, but when he saw the commotion beyond the ridge he needed no encouragement to join them with gun in hand, ready to repel a possible attack.

But Dalton, despite his assurance when he'd spoken to Virgil, wasn't sure that an attack would come. If the men were the Spitzer gang, it would suggest they had been followed intentionally into a trap. But he hadn't seen the Spitzer gang since they'd run them off, and if it hadn't been for his predicament, he'd have taken their presence as a hopeful indicator of his having chosen a passable route.

But whether the following men were trouble or not, he was relieved that they'd headed into the straight stretch of valley at just the right time to give him an excuse that would cover up his bad directions.

When the last wagon had passed him, Dalton and five other men remained and they hurried on foot along the ridge and hunkered down on the edge of the tree-line. From there, Dalton could see the river flowing down the steep ascent for several miles, but could see no sign of the riders.

Nobody worried about this, and Virgil murmured the opinion that this provided further evidence that these men *were* following them and were keeping themselves hidden. Dalton viewed Virgil's ready suspicion with some surprise, judging that he almost expected an attack.

Virgil ordered them to spread out. He and Jacob stayed on the edge of the trees, two men headed into the trees, and Loren and Dalton took up positions on clear land near the river.

They lay down on a wide and flat rock that would cover them from anyone looking their way from below provided they didn't make any sudden movements that would let anyone see them against the sky.

For ten minutes they remained quiet, until Loren spoke up.

'So, John Stanton,' he said, still keeping his gaze down-river, 'you led us into this dead end to escape these men, did you?'

Dalton again caught Loren's emphasis on his full name. He hadn't heard him use anyone else's full name, but he responded as if the question had no sinister intent.

'Like I told Virgil, I ain't taking no chances.'

'That's good to hear, John Stanton.'

Dalton took a deep breath. 'We're all friends here, Loren Steele. You can call me John.'

'Obliged, John. . . .'

Dalton waited for Loren to complete his adopted name, but even when it didn't come, the implied accusation still hung in the air. That intent could be real and Loren could have reason to suspect his identity was false, or it could just be his own guilt worrying him.

Either way, Dalton tried to keep his concern quiet, but as the long minutes passed, he found he had to give voice to that concern.

'You got a problem with me?' he asked, keeping his tone calm.

'Why you ask?'

'The way you say my name. It strikes me that you don't like me.'

'You really want me to answer that?'

'Yeah, and quit answering everything I ask with another question.'

Loren laughed with a single low snort, then shuffled back from the edge of the rock to lie looking up at Dalton.

'Then I'll say it, but I don't know how to speak without asking a question.'

Dalton shuffled back to lie beside Virgil.

'Then just say it.'

Loren took a full minute to answer, during which time Dalton noted where his horse was. If Loren was about to reveal that he knew he wasn't John Stanton, he reckoned he could slug Loren's jaw, disarm him, reach his horse,

59

and gallop away before anyone could stop him.

'Are you. . . ?' Loren rubbed his jaw, rocking his head from side to side as Dalton flexed his fist behind his back. 'Are you pursuing Eliza Boone?'

The question was so unexpected that Dalton flinched back.

'Eliza!' he spluttered, then glanced down the ridge towards Virgil, who put a finger to his lips. Dalton lowered his voice. 'What you mean?'

'I mean that as I might get me the hankering to stay with these settlers when they get to where you're leading them, I've been looking at who's here. But there ain't much in the way of unaccompanied women here.'

'Except Eliza.'

'Yeah. And you've been looking at her a lot.' Loren smiled. 'And no matter what other people say about me, I ain't a man to take another man's woman.'

Dalton hadn't realized he had been watching Eliza a lot, but he searched Loren's clear eyes, seeing no hint in them that this question was anything but honest.

'Then I'll tell you the truth. I don't know. Sometimes we're friendly, but most of time we ain't. So, I guess she's free and I won't stand in your way just as you won't stand in my way.' Dalton glanced over his shoulder towards the trees, then leaned towards Loren. 'Jacob Wade might think otherwise, but he ain't got much to offer beyond an ability to throw horseshoes. You can deal with him.'

Loren laughed. 'Obliged for your understanding, John Stanton.'

Dalton shuffled to the edge of the rock to peer down the valley.

'John, please.'

Loren joined him. 'Then John it is, John.'

With that, they settled themselves to look down the side of the ridge.

An hour passed with still no sign of anyone approaching. Loren remained resolute in his surveying of the valley below, but Dalton noticed that the men to his side were glancing amongst each other and muttering. Eventually Virgil called those men into a huddle and murmured instructions, then hurried over the ridge, doubled over, to join Dalton and Loren.

'You sure we were being followed?' he asked, drawing Dalton back from the edge. 'Nobody else has seen these men.'

'I'm sure that at least two riders were behind us and making no attempt to get closer.'

Virgil nodded. 'And once we've found out what they want and seen them off, how far do we have to backtrack to get back on the right trail?'

'Several miles.'

'I'm guessing it's a few more than that. We've probably lost a whole day with this detour.'

'Better to lose a day than risk an attack from the Spitzer gang.'

Virgil didn't reply immediately, and when he did, his voice was low.

'You may be right, but that wasn't your decision. I guess you're used to making decisions for yourself, and when you're on your own like you were down by the creek, you make damn fine ones. But you wasn't on your own here and you got to accept that if you got a problem, you come to me.' Virgil slapped his own chest. 'I'm in charge here and I'll decide what to do.'

Dalton considered mentioning that Virgil wasn't strictly in charge, but as his own position was precarious, he shrugged.

'You'll get no argument there, but what would you have done?'

'I'd have stayed on the right route and not lost us a whole day.' Virgil raised himself to look down the river, then sighed. 'But now that we have lost that time, I choose to stay here and wait them out. But that was my decision, not yours. Understand?'

Dalton raised his hands, smiling. 'You won't get any more misunderstandings from me. The moment I have a problem, I'll come to you.'

Virgil patted Dalton's back, then ran, doubled over, back to the tree-line.

Dalton watched him leave, then settled down, but he saw that Loren continued to look at Virgil.

'I got me a pebble in my boot,' he said, 'you reckon I should ask him what to do about it?'

'Might be wise,' Dalton said, enjoying hearing Loren support him for the first time. 'You don't want him to think you're threatening his authority.'

Loren snorted. 'Authority is earned and he ain't earning mine.'

'You not approve of his tactics?'

'Of course I don't. You don't sit around waiting for an attack. You make sure that an attack doesn't happen in the first place.'

Dalton was considering how he could ask what Loren's tactics would be without showing that he didn't have any better plans of his own, when he saw movement down the valley. He pointed.

Loren rose slightly to look down the valley. A half-mile down the slope two men were riding through the trees. They were taking a route that kept them hidden from casual sight, but which would still let them cover distance at a reasonable rate.

Dalton slipped back from the edge of the slope and with a few hand-gestures conveyed what was happening to the others.

Virgil nodded, then beckoned for all the men to join him.

When everyone had grouped together, he whispered quick instructions to two of his men to take up positions fifty yards down the slope. There, they would hide and wait until the riders had passed them.

Then, he ordered, they would surround these men and subdue them with warning gunfire. They would use deadly fire only if forced to.

His men hurried off to carry out their instructions as Virgil and Jacob spread out along the ridge, leaving Loren and Dalton in the middle and directly ahead of the route the riders would take.

Dalton noted Loren's firm jaw and the set of his thin lips.

'Orders ain't getting much better, are they?'

'Nope. And I ain't getting myself killed for that man.' Loren shuffled closer. 'What you expect these men to do?'

'It depends on whether they know the area. If they don't, they're just following us. If they do, they won't take kindly to us surrounding them.'

Loren nodded, his quick smile signifying that Dalton had summed up his own misgivings; then, along with Dalton, he lowered his head and kept quiet.

Down the slope the two riders closed. Dalton slowly discerned their faces. He had caught only fleeting glimpses of the bandits before, but these men had broadly the same build and, on balance, he reckoned it was highly likely that they were the same men.

He glanced at Loren, the slight narrowing of his eyes conveying his concern. In response Loren shuffled down, his gun aimed firmly down the slope.

At a steady pace the two riders passed the point where Virgil's men had slipped into hiding, then headed for the brow of the ridge.

Dalton looked past them and saw the two defenders raise themselves from hiding, but even before they'd stood up one of the riders swirled round in the saddle. The defenders had been right behind him and Dalton could see no way that he should have seen or heard them, but as the bandit threw a hand towards his rifle, Virgil jumped up.

'Fire!' he shouted.

The men down the slope and at the top of the ridge fired a barrage of warning shots, the lead tearing into tree-trunks a few feet above the bandits' heads.

'What you—' one bandit shouted, but Virgil cut him off with a stentorian command.

'Put those hands were I can see them or die where you stand!'

The riders glanced at each other and an unspoken message passed between them. Then they yanked their reins to the side and hurried through the trees, disappearing from view in a matter of seconds.

Several wild shots hurtled back through the trees from them and Virgil's men loosed off several rounds in return, but with nothing to aim at but trees, Virgil quickly shouted out an order to desist. Then he directed Jacob to head back to the wagons and find out what had happened to everyone.

As Loren slapped the earth before him in irritation at their getting away, Dalton leaned to him.

'At least Virgil proved they ain't friendly,' he said.

Loren snorted a hollow laugh. 'At least that.'

When the men from further down the slope arrived, Virgil directed everyone to take up defensive positions in an arc which would stand between the wagon train and the forest. Already, Jacob had reached the wagons and men were peeling out to take up positions before the wagons.

Virgil and the other two men hurried off to join them, and Dalton moved to follow, but Loren slapped a hand on his arm, halting him.

'I've had enough of following Virgil's orders,' he said, 'and I guess you have too. I ain't sitting out in the open for the rest of the day waiting for those bandits to attack. Are you with me, John Stanton?'

'Sure am, Loren Steele.'

'Then come on. Let's find out what they want the proper way.'

Loren winked and without further discussion they hurried down the slope, then swung round to follow the men. Even with the undergrowth being dense and the trees being tightly packed, on foot they made good speed and, at first, the trail the men had made as they brushed through the undergrowth was easy to follow.

After following for around 200 yards they found the bandits' abandoned steeds. But Loren declared that they'd then head off on a route that would run parallel to the river and which would bring them out somewhere near and above the wagons – the ideal place to launch an attack.

Fuelled on by a need to head them off, they sped off, running with large strides and vaulting fallen trees. They made too much noise for a stealthy approach but they didn't dare risk not reaching the bandits before they attacked the wagons.

Their wild chase soon caused them to lose all signs of the trail they'd been following. Dalton slowed to look around for further signs of the men's passage, but that let Loren take the lead.

Dalton could see no hints in the dense forest of the right direction to take and the tightly packed trees limited his vision to a dozen yards or so. If he had been on his own, he had no doubt he'd have become lost within minutes.

But Loren knew exactly where to go and he weaved around trees and ducked under branches with Dalton trailing in his wake. Then he took a rapid turn and set off in a different direction, the move so sudden that Dalton kept running for several strides, then had to slide to a halt and resume chasing after him.

Their general route was always uphill and whether Loren could see or hear something Dalton couldn't, or was just guessing, Dalton didn't know. But one thing was certain, Loren knew where he was going and Dalton could only hurtle after him as if he were chasing Loren and not the two bandits.

A few paces behind Loren, Dalton continually peered ahead, looking out for their quarry and he noticed a lightening ahead first, but when he found the source of the lightness, it was with a shock. One moment, they were brushing through undergrowth. The next, they emerged on to bare land.

Loren slid to a halt, Dalton ploughing into his back and pushing him forward a pace, but then they both danced back, wheeling their arms in sudden panic.

They were high, the ground was stony, and they were just a few feet away from the edge of a sheer drop of around a hundred feet. Around them, fallen trees awaited wind or gravity to drag them to the bottom. Below were the wagons, a line of men kneeling and looking away from them and towards the direction from which they expected an attack. And none of them was expecting that attack to come from higher up the sheer rock face.

Dalton bent at the waist and opened his mouth to shout a warning to them, but then a gunshot sounded, the lead winging a few inches past his hat. Dalton just had enough time to see the people below swing round to look up, but then he leapt to the ground to lie behind a fallen trunk, searching for the direction of the shooter.

The few feet of rock snaked around the top of the ridge on either side of him with the trees a solid curtain on one side and the drop on the other, but Dalton couldn't see the men. He glanced at Loren lying beside him and he returned a shake of the head.

On their bellies, they shuffled back into the trees, only one more shot scything past them. Then he and Loren crouched down between two fallen trees.

'At least everyone knows where they are,' Loren said.

'Yeah, but we could do with knowing exactly where they are or we won't be able to do nothing.'

Loren considered. 'They won't sit around waiting for us

to find them. They'll come for us, and we have to be some-where unexpected.'

'And where. . . ?'

Dalton didn't complete his question as Loren backed up his theory with a staggering level of confidence. He stood and backed out of the trees to stand in full view on the stony stretch of land. Then he hurried along the edge of the drop.

Dalton wavered, fearing Loren would pay for his theory with lead, but no gunfire came and Dalton accepted that somehow Loren had read the bandits' tactics with surpris-ing accuracy. He followed him, slipping along the edge of the sheer drop and jumping over fallen trees until he reached Loren.

His colleague had stopped in the gap between three fallen trees. Loren knelt down nearer the tree-line and Dalton lay down by the edge.

He glanced over the side, noticing that below, the defenders were looking up and had trained guns on this ledge. And the slope here was less steep than elsewhere. It was still almost precipitous, but most of the slope was climbable, and several men were venturing upwards in a quest to help them.

Dalton gestured down with a calming hand signal, signi-fying that they had some control over the situation, but Loren slapped a hand on his arm, beckoning him to lie flat.

Dalton did as ordered and looked out through the gap between two of the trees.

Further along the ledge a man was venturing out at the precise place where they had been hiding a few moments ago and was looking around.

Loren and Dalton exchanged a glance and swung their guns on to the log before them, waiting until he presented a clear target. The man loitered on the edge of the trees, standing with his back to a tree and glancing around. But then he slipped around that tree to look in their direction and Loren and Dalton ensured he paid for his mistake.

Together, they loosed off a volley of shots. Several peeled bark away, but at least two slammed into the man's chest rocking him back on his heels and knocking him into the tree. He took a stumbling pace, keeled over to his knees, then fell, clutching his chest, over the side of the ledge and disappeared from view.

Dalton heard several cries of alarm from below as the people at the bottom saw the man fall. He heard a thud as the man hit the ground, but then a gunshot pealed out. Both Loren and Dalton swirled round, their guns swinging to the side as they searched for the man who had fired.

And that man emerged from the trees, just ten feet in front of them, and fired down at them. The shot scythed into rock and hurtled away as Dalton and Loren scrambled for better cover behind the logs.

Flat on their bellies and with their senses alert for any movement, they edged out to look for the man, but he had returned to cover. Long seconds passed with Dalton darting his glance back and forth, but no further gunfire came.

Loren and Dalton exchanged silent glances, signifying and confirming with their eyes where they reckoned the man was. And that was standing behind one of the trees in front of them. The trees were just far enough apart for a man to slip through as long as he kept his elbows in, and that meant he could move to new cover in a fraction of a second.

Except they didn't know which tree he was hiding behind and he knew exactly where they were. Dalton aimed his gun at chest-height at the nearest tree while Loren aimed at the one to the side and they waited for the man to show himself.

Dalton, with his heightened senses, trusted himself to fire on pure instinct the moment the man ventured out, but with no hint as to which tree he was hiding behind, the waiting preyed on his nerves. He started to wonder whether the man could have sought different cover while they had been diving for their lives.

He glanced at Loren, who darted a glance back, his raised eyebrows confirming that he also thought this man wouldn't have the patience to wait this long.

And that did it for Dalton. Loren's hunches had been right so far and he decided to back this one. He stood slowly. Loren saw his intent and nodded with a short gesture, then paced over the logs to stand outside them. Then he took a long pace to the side, walking sideways, aiming to get a different angle on the trees and bring the man into view.

He took another pace, his view of the trees shifting and letting him see behind the trunks, but the man was still not visible. He took another pace. Still he didn't appear and, from this angle, Dalton reckoned he ought to be able to see him.

Dalton winced. The man couldn't be where he expected him to be. He glanced at Loren, but he was swinging his gun round to aim at Dalton's head.

For one shocked moment, Dalton thought his worst fears were justified, that Loren had really known his true identity and was about to kill him. But Loren fired, the slug hurtling over Dalton's shoulder, a cry emerging from behind him.

Dalton turned on his heel, seeing the blur of a man leaping at him before he piled into his side. Dalton just had time to note that he must have been lying behind one of the fallen logs. Then they wheeled backwards.

On the very edge of the slope Dalton dug his heels in and slid to a halt. He and the man stared into each other's eyes, the man's eyes glazing from Loren's possibly terminal gunshot.

Then Dalton saw a flash of metal as the man swung his gun up to aim at his chest. But his injury had slowed him, giving Dalton time to react more quickly. He swung his gun round and tore a shot low into his assailant's stomach at point-blank range.

The man folded and swayed backwards, but then a shot from behind hammered into him and he rocked forward to fall against Dalton, pushing him back.

Dalton scrambled for purchase, but he was on the edge of the slope. Pebbles and stones slipped away from his questing feet. Loren shouted something to him as the man, with his last dying action, hurled his arms around Dalton's chest and collapsed.

Dalton's trailing heel landed on air and he tumbled backwards, the man's dead weight dragging him down. Dalton hurled his arms wide, reaching for something to grab, but he was already too far from the edge and, as he rolled round to face downwards, below was the terrible long drop to the wagons.

CHAPTER 6

Dalton blinked groggily as his surroundings swayed and swirled around him, then focused.

He was lying under cover in a wagon, and by the look of the stored furniture, it was Henry's. A cold towel lay on his bare chest. He moved to rise but a wave of nausea hit him and forced him to flop back onto his back.

'Don't move,' a voice said beside him. 'You got hurt.'

Dalton needed a moment before he worked out that Henry Boone had spoken. He let his head roll to the side to look at him.

'What happened?'

'Didn't see it myself but from the way everyone tells it, you and Loren sneaked up on the Spitzer gang. But one of them took you down with him and you both came hurtling down to us, going head over heels. You sure had plenty of luck to avoid breaking every bone in your body.'

'Yeah, I sure had plenty of luck.'

'And you had plenty more in ending up in here. Eliza is a fine carer.' Henry winked. 'But you could have found an easier way to win her heart.'

'What you mean?'

'I mean getting yourself all beat up just so she can look

72

after you. It's sneaky, but it's sure to work.'

Dalton joined Henry in chuckling then raised the towel to look at the purple bruises beneath. He winced and dropped it back on his chest, but the towel slid off his chest and to the floor.

Dalton muttered to himself then rooted round for it, but only succeeded in knocking over Henry's chest and tumbling the town sign in the folded blanket to the floor. Dalton flopped back on his bedding and prepared himself for rescuing the mess, but Eliza poked her head into the wagon, then climbed inside.

She stood hunched with her hands on her hips, surveying the damage.

'I thought you'd be one of those fools who wouldn't lie down and rest.' She picked up the sign and righted the chest. 'But I didn't think you'd wreck the wagon while you were busy being stupid.'

She continued to complain but Dalton lay back, enjoying her chiding of him. When she'd fussed around him, he pointed out of the back of the wagon.

'Have we moved on?'

'No. We're staying here for the night. So you can rest and concentrate on getting well. I do not want to waste any more time than I have to looking after the likes of you.'

'You don't have to do this at all.'

She pointed a firm finger at him. 'Do not tempt me.'

Dalton glanced at Henry, who narrowed his eyes, suggesting he should change the subject. So, he nodded down at his chest.

'How bad is it?'

'You'll be fine. You didn't break any bones.' She considered his chest. 'But you got some bad bruising, and not all of it from the fall.'

Dalton glanced down, seeing that the faded yellow bruises from Vaughn's beatings still marred his exposed skin.

'I guess I've seen some trouble before.'

'How did you hurt your wrists?'

Dalton fingered the band of bruises around his left wrist, the remnants of two weeks spent in cuffs, then looked up, but saw only openness in her gaze and nothing other than a desire to make conversation.

'Can't remember,' Dalton said, avoiding creating a complex lie that might cause him problems later.

'Then don't think too much. You had a nasty bang on the head.'

'Yeah, but I need to show everyone where to go.'

Dalton rubbed his brow as he searched for the best way to word an excuse that the bang on his head had affected his memory, but Eliza shook her head.

'You don't need to worry about directing us for a while. Sheriff Melrose from Applegate arrived. He was after the Spitzer gang, but he's staying with us to show us where to go.' She turned to leave the wagon. 'And when you're fit enough to talk, he wants to speak to you.'

Dalton listened to the early morning bird-song. Last night he had slept fitfully, partly because he couldn't find a way to lie comfortably, and partly because of his concern about an impending encounter with Sheriff Melrose.

He couldn't believe that the lawman wouldn't know the real John Stanton, so his new identity was sure to come to an inglorious end within seconds of meeting him.

He had helped this group and saved lives. So, they

would speak up for him, but he couldn't think of a story that would explain his actions before joining the wagons that wouldn't draw attention to the dead bodies back beside the river. Melrose had probably never heard of Deputy Vaughn and Dalton, but no matter what story he accepted, it would look bad for him.

Henry was still sleeping beside him as Dalton decided he had to get away from the wagon train. When he'd been Vaughn's prisoner he'd vowed that he'd sooner die than be anyone's prisoner again and even if he had little chance of evading the lawman in his injured state, he had to try.

He rolled from his bedding and knelt, flexing his back. Muscles complained, confirming that riding would be uncomfortable, but he gritted his teeth and slipped into his shirt, then jacket. The weight on his skin chafed his bruises and scrapes, but he reckoned he'd have to get used to it.

After nodding a farewell to the sleeping Henry, he slipped out of the wagon and glanced around. Nobody had risen from their slumbers yet; all the wagons were closed and quiet. Loren slept outside but was out of view.

Over at the edge of the ridge two men sat huddled, staring down the river, the only approach to this location. He watched them, reckoning that keeping watch at this time was a thankless task and, from the men's unmoving postures, they were probably dozing in a semi-conscious state.

He'd alert them when he headed downriver, but he could excuse his actions by explaining that he was scouting around. When he failed to return, they would raise the alarm, but that would give him several hours in which to find a place to hole up.

He didn't want to risk spending time searching for food, reckoning that a gun and a horse was pretty much all he needed. So he headed for his horse, shuffling past the line of wagons with short paces, but when he passed the last wagon, he flinched. A man was sitting back against the sheer rock face and watching him, a blanket drawn up to his chin.

The man stood, the blanket fell away, and Dalton couldn't help but notice the star on his chest.

'You shouldn't push yourself too much,' Sheriff Melrose said. 'You took a bad fall.'

'I got a job to do,' Dalton said, deciding that making a run for his horse was impossible, but detecting no suspicion in Melrose's tone.

'I can see that. I'd heard about you, John, but I always took you to be an older man.'

Dalton limited himself to a smile, fighting to avoid revealing the wave of relief that overcame him.

'And I'd heard about you. I always took you for a younger man.'

Melrose provided a relaxed laugh and went to the back of the last wagon. He took a ladle from beside the water barrel, filled it and held it out to Dalton, who took advantage of Melrose's assumption that he had been looking for sustenance and drained the ladle.

'I won't keep you outside for long,' Melrose said. 'But I just need to hear what happened from your viewpoint.'

'No problem.'

While dunking the ladle, he covered the details in a matter-of-fact manner. Melrose nodded frequently. When Dalton had finished he wandered around in a small circle, rubbing his chin and considering.

'But why bring the wagons here? I'd figure you'd head through Green Pass. That's a far easier route than any other.'

'And we will go that way now. When I saw we were being followed, I came here to make a stand. If I had been on my own, I'd have doubled back and taken care of the problem, but . . .' Dalton shrugged, then took another gulp of water and returned the ladle to the barrel. 'Perhaps I did wrong, but it's hard to know what's right when you're protecting the lives of this many people.'

'I understand the problem. And I guess it's what I might have done in the same situation.' Melrose turned to his blanket, but then glanced back at him. 'You need to rest, but can I ask you one more thing?'

'Go on,' Dalton said. He steeled himself for what might prove to be a tricky question as Melrose drew him away from the last wagon.

'I've never heard of Loren Steele, so I didn't ask him this – what impression have you formed of these people?'

'They're decent, hard-working families looking to start a new life.'

Melrose nodded, his downcast eyes suggesting he was debating whether to ask another question.

'Any of them strike you as being less decent than the others?'

'What you getting at?'

Melrose sighed. 'I intend to stay with you a while longer, but I'd prefer it if you kept this to yourself. The men who attacked you *were* the Spitzer gang, four men led by two gunslinger brothers, Fritz and Herman.'

'Only two men attacked us.'

'And that means the other two are still out there – and they're the brothers, the worst of the bunch.'

Dalton rubbed his ribs. 'Don't worry. As soon as I'm fit enough, I'll help you defend everyone against them.'

'I know you will, but I didn't join you because I was after them. Someone beat Marcus Wilcox, a snake-oil seller from Applegate, to death in a frenzied attack. Certain facts suggest that someone on this wagon train killed him.'

Dalton looked away as he considered, then shook his head.

'These people are decent men and women. Are you sure the Spitzer gang didn't kill him?'

'I thought it was them at first. Marcus had a thousand dollars on him and whoever killed him stole it. Everything pointed to the Spitzer gang, except they had a real alibi, for once. But this wagon train left town on the day of the murder, and I reckon the Spitzer gang followed you because they'd worked out someone here stole that thousand dollars.'

'I ain't questioning your actions, but that don't sound like much of a reason to follow us for a week.'

'Like I said – certain other facts point to the culprit being with this wagon train.'

'And you won't tell me what those facts are.' Dalton considered Melrose's impassive face, then shrugged. 'You could search the wagons for the money, I guess.'

'And I might find it, but that won't prove nothing. When people like me ask difficult questions, groups like this have a habit of providing excuses for each other. And in my experience, it's the newcomers like you and Loren who often take the blame.'

Dalton provided a rueful smile. 'Yeah, I know that.'

Dalton looked away towards the gorge as he considered his dealings with these people. He'd been more worried about anyone discovering his real identity than looking out for anyone else acting suspiciously. But nobody had given him cause for concern – except one – although his dispute with Jacob had been on a personal level. Then Dalton remembered something Jacob had said.

'You've just thought of somebody,' Melrose said, interrupting Dalton's thoughts. 'Don't keep your suspicions to yourself. I'll do the thinking while you get these people over the mountains.'

'Then I'd suggest Jacob Wade. He said something to me . . .' Dalton sighed, his sudden suspicion not sounding quite so damning now that he was voicing it. 'It was probably nothing, but he told me that soon he'd impress someone. Perhaps that means he's stolen a thousand dollars.'

'It could. Anything more?'

'No, I don't . . .' Dalton glanced away, another thought coming to him now that he was considering the Wade family's actions in a suspicious light. 'His father has acted oddly, too. I'm guessing it took some effort to catch up with us.'

'It did.'

'That's because Virgil has pushed us to cover as many miles as we can each day.'

Melrose nodded. 'And that means he's either eager to get to where he's going, or eager to get away from where he's been.'

'Yeah.' Dalton shrugged. 'But when you think like that, everybody's actions could be suspicious, even mine.'

Melrose laughed. 'And with your reputation, you're the only person here I do trust. Obliged for the information.'

Dalton smiled and moved to turn away, then turned back.

'One other thing, if you wouldn't mind.' Dalton rubbed his chest and winced. 'But I could do with some rest. Could you direct them for a while?'

'No problem. I assume you were heading up Green Pass, around the bluff, keeping below the ridge and then over Blind Man's Canyon.'

'It's the best way to go,' Dalton said, keeping his expression blank.

'Then I'll take them as far as the canyon.' Melrose smiled. 'And you'll be pleased to hear I'm planning to see your old friends Eddy and Tucker Malone there.'

Dalton raised his eyebrows and put on a smile.

'That's good news. What you seeing them about?'

'They left a message that they knew something about Marcus Wilcox's murder, but when I got back to Applegate, they'd headed off to disappear down another glory-hole in the canyon. You know what they're like.' Melrose leaned forward and lowered his voice. 'We'll have to hope that your friends will be able to tell me something I can use when we get there.'

As the wagons headed up the pass that John Stanton would have known about, Dalton devoted his resting time to thinking. Based on Melrose's estimate of their likely speed, he had four days to get well enough to leave the wagon train, or find a way to avoid meeting Tucker and Eddy Malone.

However much he tried, Dalton couldn't think of a plausible excuse to be away during that meeting, but as regards returning to health, he improved faster than he expected.

Eliza was a bountiful source of energy. She maintained a matter-of-fact demeanour, neither engaging in casual conversation nor spending a moment longer with him than she needed to. But Dalton got the impression from her terse comments and gentle chiding that she enjoyed seeing one of her patients improve and that their enforced intimacy of a sort was helping to patch over their previous misunderstanding.

With her devoting as much time to caring for him as she did to her father, after just two days Dalton felt that he was fit enough to leave the wagon and pace around.

So when they settled down that night he rolled from his bedding and flexed his back before he stood. His back was still sore and complained with every movement, but at least he could move around freely and he reckoned he'd be able to ride in the next day or so.

Outside, he heard voices, which he assumed were Eliza and Newell, but when he emerged from the wagon he found it was Eliza and Jacob. Their tones implied a casual conversation and Jacob's posture suggested he had been passing and had just stopped, but they both silenced and turned to him. Eliza smiled. Jacob did not.

'Good to see you're mending,' Jacob said with nothing in his blank tone suggesting he was being honest.

'Thanks to Eliza,' Dalton said. He nodded to her, then looked around. Loren was leaning back against the next wagon, looking straight ahead. He raised his voice. 'And I'd have probably died without Loren's help.'

Jacob snorted, his sneer confirming that he wasn't exactly pleased with the result of Loren's bravery. But Dalton had no interest in his petulance and continued to look at Loren, noting that although most of the people had looked in on him while he'd been resting, Jacob and Loren were the only people who hadn't. Jacob's failure to see him he could understand, but after facing danger together, he thought Loren and he should have reached an understanding.

While Loren continued to avoid looking at him, Eliza fussed around him, checking his bandages and admonishing him for leaving the wagon without her permission.

Jacob watched Eliza's attention leave him with his upper lip curled back in a sneer. In response, Dalton wriggled and murmured a few comments to prolong the time she'd spend with him.

When she'd finished, Eliza declared that he was well enough to go on a short walk. She also stated that she needed water for Henry. She looked at a bucket standing beside Dalton. Then she looked at each man in turn, but neither man moved. With a snort she moved to grab the bucket to fetch the water herself. But that encouraged Jacob to hurry past her and lunge for the bucket.

Dalton had caught Eliza's hint, but he didn't want to risk carrying anything heavy yet. Then, seeing Jacob moving, he also lunged. The sudden movement sent a bolt of pain ripping through his back but he still clamped a hand on the bucket first. He stood, stooped, wondering whether he could straighten his back. Taking advantage of the delay, Jacob also grabbed the handle and the two men tugged.

'Stop it, you two,' Eliza said. 'I'll get the water myself.'

Dalton raised his eyes to look at Jacob and the two men locked gazes. Dalton was the first to raise his hand.

Jacob grinned, but then his eyes glazed, perhaps as he

realized that going on an errand would find favour with Eliza but give Dalton time to be alone with her. He snapped his hand up and straightened.

With plenty of low muttering about all men being idiots, Eliza slipped between them and took the bucket herself, then headed away.

'So,' Jacob said, 'it seems neither of us is fetching the water.'

Dalton straightened slowly. 'Maybe next time we'll get to decide once and for all who'll fetch things for her.'

'Maybe we will, but I know who that person will be. And I reckon you do too.'

'Yeah.' Dalton turned to climb back into the wagon, finding that the thought of going for a short walk had now turned sour. 'I do.'

Jacob slammed a hand on Dalton's shoulder and swung him round. In his weakened state, the action bent Dalton double.

'And we both know we got a fight coming to us, John.' Jacob flexed his fist. 'Now might be the right time for it.'

Dalton stayed bent double while he confirmed that Jacob's sudden action hadn't hurt him, then looked up. Jacob had raised his fists and his blazing eyes said he wasn't in the mood for placating words. Before he'd sustained his injuries, Dalton would have retaliated but in his present state, he wouldn't be able to provide a good account of himself, and Jacob knew it.

'Soon, Jacob, soon, but not today.'

'I knew you were a yellow-belly.' Jacob hurled back his fist ready to pummel Dalton, who flinched away, a hand rising to ward off a blow, but it never came.

Loren had sneaked up on Jacob. He grabbed his hand as he swung it back. He held the fist in his firm grip behind Jacob's back.

Jacob struggled, but Loren held him close to his chest, thrust his arm up in a half-Nelson, and whispered something in his ear that made Jacob gulp. Then he patted him on the head as if he was granting favour to a child, and pushed him away.

Jacob stumbled, then swirled round to glare at Loren and Dalton in turn.

'You'll pay for that now, both of you.' Then he stormed round and made off before either man could reply, leaving Dalton and Loren alone.

'Seems I'm obliged to you for saving me again,' Dalton said.

'No problem, John Stanton, no problem at all.'

Dalton continued towards the wagon, but a twinge rippled across his back and eroded his fragile good mood. He turned back.

'I thought you'd agreed to call me John,' he snapped. 'Being as we've fought side by side, I'd be obliged if you'd do that.'

Loren gave a slow nod. 'I'll do that, John. . . .'

Loren turned and headed away, but he passed the wagon that he'd previously been standing beside and continued walking. He acknowledged everyone he passed with a nod until he slipped out between two wagons. There, Sheriff Melrose was sitting and he passed by him, then continued for twenty paces before stopping to look up at the route ahead.

Dalton raised his gaze to look in the same direction. They had now achieved some height; behind them the plains stretched away. They were heading towards a flat ridge of land between two peaks, beyond which Dalton presumed they would start the downward trek. The ridge was close and Dalton was sure the estimates of their progress were right and that he had not much more than a day to find a good excuse to leave the wagon train.

He was about to climb into the wagon, but the odd nature of his confrontations since he'd come outside tapped at his thoughts. He could understand why Jacob didn't like him, but Loren hadn't appeared friendly either. Loren had claimed that he was interested in Eliza, but he had *done* nothing to suggest that that was the case and unless Loren was being devious in his courting, Dalton didn't believe that excuse.

As he had more worrying matters to deal with, he could leave the issue unresolved but, for a reason he couldn't fathom, he didn't like the idea that a man who was as resourceful as Loren didn't like him. So, instead of climbing into the wagon he followed him, acknowledging the people he passed with nods and the occasional short chat about his improving condition.

Sheriff Melrose smiled at him as he passed and he continued until he joined Loren, who despite the fifteen minutes it'd taken Dalton to reach him, was still staring up at the route ahead.

They stood silently for a minute. Loren was the first to speak.

'Would you have chosen this route, John?' he asked, looking at the low ridge between the peaks.

'I would.'

'And how many times have you headed over Blind

Man's Canyon and the ridge beyond, John?'

Dalton looked over Loren's shoulder, seeing that Sheriff Melrose was out of hearing-range, but near enough to detect any friction between them. He guessed that Loren had chosen this spot for precisely that reason.

'Time for some straight talking, Loren,' he said. 'We fought together against the Spitzer gang, but you never came to see me afterwards.'

'Didn't want to bother a man who was getting himself all fixed up.'

'Then I'm obliged for your consideration.' Dalton took a deep breath. 'But you claimed you had an interest in Eliza, yet you don't even talk to her.'

'Not all of us care to make fools of ourselves squabbling with kids over buckets of water.'

Dalton glanced away, wondering whether to push this matter, but he was sure Loren was hiding something and this was an ideal time to find out what it was.

'Loren, just tell it to me straight. Why don't you like me?'

Loren turned from his consideration of the landscape to look at Dalton.

'Why think that? I saved your life, didn't I?'

'You did, but I don't reckon that means what it ought to mean.'

Loren rubbed his jaw, then swung away to look around.

'So, you really want to hear it, do you, with Sheriff Melrose just a few paces away?'

'He's far enough away. He can't hear us, as you intended when you stood here. So, no more questions, no more insinuations, no more snide comments, no more avoiding my questions. If you got something to say, just say it.'

'All right.' Loren looked deep into Dalton's eyes, his craggy features hardening to solid iron. 'Who are you and what have you done with John Stanton?'

CHAPTER 7

Ever since Loren had joined the wagon train, Dalton had half-expected that he would unmask him, but he still couldn't stop himself gulping. But Loren hadn't mentioned his suspicion to anyone else and there had to be a reason for that, so he decided to answer honestly.

He placed a hand on Loren's shoulder and led him away from the wagons, smiling. Loren returned the smile in case anyone was looking at them. A hundred yards from the wagons, Dalton stopped and stood square on to Loren.

'My name is of no importance,' he said, 'and I've done nothing to John Stanton.'

'Then where is he?'

'I won't lie. I'm sorry, but he's buried back beside the river.'

Loren's right eye flickered with a momentary twinge, this being his only reaction.

'You kill him?'

'Nope. He saved my life.'

'And you're repaying his memory by pretending to be him.' Loren snorted. 'If you knew the man he was, you'd know how pathetic that is.'

'I only knew him for a few minutes, but I know you're right.'

'And that's the first thing you've said I do believe, Dalton.'

Dalton sighed. 'So, you already knew who I was.'

'Yeah. I asked around. It didn't take long before I heard the story of the dead outlaw and the lawman.'

'Then why avoid confronting me with your suspicions?'

'I just wanted to know how long it'd take you to tell the truth.'

'And with a lawman so close, you must know how hard it was for me to tell you that. And that must prove things ain't what they seem.'

With this admission, Loren looked aloft and his shoulders relaxed.

'There's always a chance of that.' He sighed, his glazed eyes suggesting he was recalling old and fond memories. 'I knew John some years back. When I heard he was leading these people, I reckoned I'd ride along with him awhile and swap some old tales. Except he's dead and you're pretending to be him. You must see why I got suspicious.'

'I do, but why didn't you tell Melrose?'

'John would have known. Out here, you're on your own and you make your own justice. So, I'll tell you this – I ain't interested in hearing no lies, but I will work out what happened to John and, if necessary, I'll deliver my own justice in my own way.' Loren slapped his holster and narrowed his eyes. 'Don't bother watching your back, Dalton, because I'm watching it for you.'

Loren turned away, but Dalton clamped a hand on his shoulder and halted him.

'And I ain't interested in hearing no lies either. You

didn't tell Melrose about your suspicions, not because you want to deal with me, but because you don't want Melrose to learn of my suspicions about you.'

Loren sneered. 'You got nothing.'

'The Spitzer gang were following us and you knew what they'd do, where they'd go, and how to stop them. And that means you've met them before, except you didn't mention that.'

'And why does that matter?'

'It matters because it means you didn't join us to meet an old friend, but for some other reason, and I reckon it had something to do with why Sheriff Melrose is here. So, Loren, don't watch your back because I'm watching it for you.'

Dalton raised his hand and let Loren pace away, shaking his head. He watched him leave, then turned to look at the ridge.

For the day after Dalton's encounter with Loren, the wagon train snaked up several passes at a steady pace. Dalton felt stronger than he had the previous day, but not strong enough to ride and he sat up in the wagon, pondering his complicated situation.

Sheriff Melrose did call in on him to confirm that he was taking the best route and Dalton could only nod while silently noting that if he had still been directing everyone, he would have never found this route.

That night they negotiated the topmost pass. The ridge for which they had been heading was now just a few miles ahead, its bare and rocky length a short saddle between two snow-flecked peaks. After several days of travelling with high and steep sides protecting them from the prevailing winds, a harsh and grit-filled wind whipped around them. In a matter of minutes the temperature dropped, forcing everyone to search for extra clothing.

Tomorrow they would reach Blind Man's Canyon, and if Dalton couldn't find a reason to be elsewhere for a while, he didn't relish the thought of leaving and making his own way over such inhospitable terrain.

In the wagon, Henry Boone huddled beneath several blankets, his previous appreciation of the falling temperature having now departed.

'Tell me about Sweet Valley,' Henry said, his teeth chattering, 'and warm me up.'

Dalton winced as he lay on his back in the wagon. For most of the last few days Henry had been silent, but Dalton had been dreading that their close proximity would lead to inevitable questions he couldn't answer.

'I could,' Dalton said, 'but you have the sign. You must have a vision of what you want.'

'It's has to be a valley.' Henry chuckled. 'And it has to be mighty fine.'

'And you can put your mind at rest. It will be.' Dalton remembered something the real John Stanton had said. 'Beyond the mountains, there's land aplenty and valleys galore for anyone to start a new life.'

Henry smiled and raised himself. 'And when will we get there?'

'Not long now.' Dalton flashed a smile, but Henry's brow furrowed with the hint of another impending question and Dalton asked one of his own to deflect him. 'Why do your family and the Wades hate each other?'

Henry sighed and flopped back on his bedding.

'That is a long and painful story.'

'Then just tell me the basics.'

Henry didn't reply immediately. His breath wheezed, then he rolled his head to the side to look at Dalton.

'We moved on after the flood, but I first thought about a fresh start when both our wives died. They got a fever, throats all swelled up . . .' Henry raised a bony hand to swipe away a tear. 'Damn fever came from somewhere and at the time nobody cared about nothing but stopping it, but once it'd moved on to torture some other poor souls, we both got to thinking.'

Henry offered no more details, and Dalton spoke up.

'Virgil blamed your wife for giving the fever to his wife. . . .'

'And I blamed his. But who's to know who's to blame? And as we never will, there's no way we'll ever talk again.'

'Have you tried to make peace with him?'

'He came to see me after we'd left Applegate. He'd bought a potion to make me feel better, but it didn't and I won't suffer his company again.'

'If he was prepared to try once, perhaps you should try again while you still can, for both your families' sakes.'

'Perhaps, but how can I forgive him for what his wife did to mine?'

Dalton could think of nothing to say in response. He slipped out of the wagon. He discovered that Loren was scouting around, then asked if there was anything he could do to help. Eliza allocated him the task of collecting wood from the sparse trees, and completing this simple activity increased his confidence in his returning strength.

At Melrose's insistence the group found extra logs to take with them, Melrose providing the explanation that 'Stanton' would have advised them to do the same.

As working in the thinner air had already tired him, Dalton returned to the wagon before anyone could ask him why that might be so, and spent the night huddled up with Henry.

The next day Dalton rose early. He felt fitter than he had done for a while and, despite his predicament, a curious optimism threatened to burst out, as if he was emerging from a cocoon or a prolonged hibernation.

Melrose insisted that they set off as early as possible and Dalton decided he needed to start riding again. As Loren was at the back of the wagons, he rode beside the lawman. His bruised chest complained at first, but the rolling motion also eased the remaining soreness in his muscles.

'Learnt anything to suggest that either Virgil or Jacob Wade is guilty of killing Wilcox?' he asked by way of starting a conversation.

'Nope,' Melrose said. 'I'm putting all my hopes into Eddy and Tucker knowing something. But I'll tell you one thing for sure, I'll watch their reactions when I do ask them.'

Dalton nodded. He had been planning to steer the conversation round to the possibility that he might scout around to look for the Spitzer brothers and so not visit Blind Man's Canyon, but an alternative idea came to him.

'Perhaps you can do that before you get there.'

Melrose turned in the saddle. 'What you suggesting?'

'You've told everyone you're accompanying us but you didn't reveal the real reason. If you were to announce you're investigating the murder of Marcus Wilcox and that Eddy and Tucker know something about it, the guilty person might panic himself into doing something rash.'

Melrose rocked his head from side to side, frowning.

'If I did that, he could go after the Malone brothers. But then again, I don't think the killer will kill again. I reckon Marcus's murder was an act of rage, not malice.' Melrose nodded, beaming. 'I'd heard good things about you, and I can see they're justified.'

'Shall I think of an excuse for us to stop so you can tell everyone?'

'You're right that the sooner I say something, the sooner the killer can start worrying, but I won't do it just yet.' Melrose pointed ahead, then winked. 'And we both know where the best place to do it is, don't we?'

Dalton kept his expression blank, but when Melrose continued to smile and gave no hint as to where that place would be, Dalton slowly matched his smile, as if he'd just seen his intent.

'Yeah,' he said. 'That sure is the best place.'

Dalton then rode in silence to avoid Melrose detecting his discomfort, but he didn't have to wait long before he discovered where Melrose would try to expose the killer.

Before noon they reached the end of the flat terrain before the ridge. Throughout the morning, Dalton had assumed that this flat stretch of land would continue until they reached the ridge between the two peaks. Then they would crest the ridge to see the land beyond. He had assumed that Blind Man's Canyon would emerge beside them at some stage, but he was wrong.

When they stopped, the last ridge was just a mile or so ahead and almost level with them.

But on first glance it might as well be 1,000 miles. Between that ridge and their current position there was nothing; the ground dropped away into a deep canyon, its base lost in the mists below, the deep gash stretching away

94

on both sides seemingly for ever.

'Blind Man's Canyon,' Melrose announced to Virgil as he drew his wagon up at the edge of the sharp drop.

'What you bring us this way for?' Virgil murmured, blinking rapidly as he considered the huge drop into the canyon below.

'It's the best way.'

Virgil turned to Dalton for support, but Dalton just pointed across the canyon to the ridge opposite and smiled.

'Like he said, it's the best way. I never promised it'd be easy.'

Virgil jumped down from his wagon and shuffled to the edge, then stared ahead with his hands on his hips and his hat tipped back. But Melrose joined him and pointed to a rocky outcrop which burst out of the opposite side of the canyon.

'Don't worry. Many is the prospector who's visited that outcrop, searching for the gold they're all convinced is there.'

'So,' Virgil mused, looking down again, 'there *is* a way down.'

'For man and horses, there is. But for these wagons, we'll have to be more inventive.'

Virgil sighed. 'Then it's a good job we got plenty of rope.'

'And the logs,' Melrose said, patting his back.

By mid-afternoon, Virgil had organized the group into making a frame over which they'd lower the wagons down the side of the canyon. He looped rope over two crossed logs, with a third log anchoring the structure on the edge of the drop.

Further back from the edge, a four-horse team were tethered to a rope that wound around a series of stays hammered deep into the ground and around which the rope would slowly pass and control the wagons' descent.

Dalton had expected that Melrose would now mention the fact that when they reached the bottom he would discover who had killed Marcus Wilcox, but he said nothing.

As Dalton was apparently familiar with the terrain, Melrose suggested that he go down on foot first to secure the area below. Dalton didn't think that he could refuse but to Dalton's surprise, Loren, the only other person aside from Melrose who didn't have a wagon to protect, volunteered to go down with him.

Dalton led him to the edge of the canyon but then, without fuss, Loren took the lead. As soon as they'd disappeared over the side, he put them on a trail down the canyon side that was obvious as soon as Dalton was on it, but which wasn't visible from the top.

Dalton quickly saw that Melrose had chosen the ideal place to descend. The canyon side where they'd lower the wagons was sheer, but elsewhere a man on horseback could ride down. But he also saw that the distance they'd have to lower the wagons was considerable and was further than he thought they could cover safely.

He kept these thoughts to himself and rode behind Loren, concentrating on keeping his footing on the slippery ground. But later, he discovered that his initial fears weren't justified and that Melrose's plan was a wise one.

Approximately half-way down there was a wide ledge on to which he planned to lower the wagons. Then the settlers would have to stay there, perhaps for the night, and lower the wagons on the second stage of their journey tomorrow. That was safer than lowering them the whole distance in one go.

Loren and Dalton arrived on this ledge just as the first wagon appeared over the side of the canyon. Neither man had spoken so far and, as the wagon came down towards them, Dalton noted Loren's refusal to meet his eye. He presumed he wasn't interested in rekindling their previous argument.

From this lower position, Dalton had a clearer view of the terrain on the other side of the canyon. The route upwards was not as sheer, there being terraces that a wagon train in single file could snake up. As he waited for the first wagon to arrive, he considered various potential routes, and Loren, with no trace of sarcasm, drew his attention to one in particular.

Then they stood to the side of the ledge and guided in the approaching wagon, which landed safely. In short order they unhooked the wagon, signalled for the rope to return, and manoeuvred the wagon away.

Dalton couldn't help but notice that the first wagon had been Virgil's. Clearly, the group's assumed leader wouldn't let anyone do something he hadn't first proved to be safe and viable.

The first wagon had come down unaccompanied but, after it had proved that the technique was safe, several people joined the next wagon. Later, livestock came down until the ledge became crowded.

But the sun also set behind the peak to their side and it became clear that no matter how cramped they became, they would have to stay on this ledge for the night.

Henry's wagon came down last, with Eliza and Henry

inside, but Newell stayed back to help Sheriff Melrose and Virgil dismantle, then bring down the frame they'd built.

As soon as they arrived everyone joined them in setting up the frame for the second half of the journey. Everyone worked late into the evening to ensure that they could start on the second leg as early as possible tomorrow.

By the time they'd completed the task night had fallen. Everyone all but collapsed into exhausted huddles. A frugal cold meal was passed around and, from the frequent glances that Melrose shot Dalton's way, Dalton reckoned he was now waiting for an opportunity to use Dalton's idea in the one place from where nobody could leave.

But Melrose bided his time until the conversation around the camp-fire drifted towards a suitable point.

'So,' Virgil asked at last, turning to Melrose, 'how much longer are you staying with us?'

'I'm afraid this is as far as I can go,' Melrose said, 'but I reckon Dalton is fit enough now to direct you the rest of the way.'

'And we're most obliged that you stepped in and helped.'

'No problem. But I still wanted to come here to see these two prospectors, Eddy and Tucker Malone.' Melrose leaned back, pausing as he awaited the inevitable question.

'What was so vital you had to come all this way just to see two men?'

Melrose rubbed his brow as if he was debating whether to answer, then shrugged.

'Someone killed a snake-oil seller, Marcus Wilcox, then

stole one thousand dollars off him.'

Several people drew in their breath during the quiet that descended on the group. Dalton lowered his hat and glanced around, searching for anyone who appeared more shocked than they ought to be.

He saw Newell flinch and look up, his gaze seeking out Eliza, who also reacted in the same way. And Virgil's wide eyes and hunched posture suggested either surprise or perhaps concern as he looked at the camp-fire in the centre of the ledge.

'That's a shock,' he said.

Melrose shrugged. 'It is, and apparently, the Malone brothers in the canyon know who killed him. Tomorrow, I'll know who I have to track down.'

'And why have you only seen fit to tell us this now?'

'There wasn't no need for me to say anything.'

'There was. I need to know everything that affects this wagon train.'

'This doesn't.' Melrose leaned forward as if he was about to say something more, and perhaps that he had reason to suspect that the murder of Marcus Wilcox *did* affect this wagon train. But he said nothing more, and neither did Virgil.

The group sat in silence awhile. When someone did break the silence it was to start an unnecessary debate about the arrangements for the second leg of their journey down the side of the canyon the following day.

Melrose didn't join in this conversation and wandered off to stand on the edge of the canyon, but as he left he glanced at Dalton, who waited for a few minutes then followed.

The two men stood on the edge of the canyon, looking

out into the blackness beyond.

Melrose kept his voice low. 'The route up the side of the canyon is treacherous in the dark. The route down is treacherous in the dark. We're in the one place where nobody can come in or out and we have a killer amongst us who knows he'll be uncovered when we reach the bottom tomorrow. He'll have to do something and he'll have to do it soon.'

'Then I hope it's soon and not when we're lowering the wagons tomorrow. Desperate men can do desperate things.'

'They can, but I wouldn't have gone along with your plan if I thought he'd be that desperate. But still keep on the look-out for anyone acting oddly tonight and anyone eager to be the first to head down tomorrow.'

'Or the last.'

Melrose nodded. 'Either way, someone will leave this wagon train before we reach the bottom, and whoever that is, I'll follow him.'

Dalton sighed as he watched Melrose move to the position he'd marked out to sleep tonight.

'Yeah,' he said to himself, 'and I hope that person ain't me.'

To avoid raising concern, they'd agreed earlier that although they'd keep watch tonight, they wouldn't let anyone know what they were doing.

Dalton had chosen to stay awake first.

When everyone had settled down, he sat back against his saddle, flexing his back whenever he sat in one position for too long, and watched the moon sink towards the horizon. With their horses and livestock corralled at the back of the ledge and the wagons pressed together tightly, the ledge was still, most people choosing to sleep under cover.

Dalton noted that Loren slept apart from the group on the edge of the ledge and that Melrose slept on the other side of the wagons, close to the only route away from the ledge.

Melrose had said he slept light but had asked Dalton to relieve him when the moon set.

Dalton doubted that anyone who decided to run in the night would be able to leave quietly and he frequently let his eyes close as he dozed in fitful spells. But he came awake after one such spell to find that the moon was dipping close to the peak to his side.

He stood, stretched, then paced on a steady tour of the ledge, ensuring he didn't look as if he was deliberately visiting Melrose to check on him. He walked to the edge, looked out into the dark well of the canyon, then paced around the endmost wagon to the clear space beyond. Melrose was sleeping hunched under his blanket, either sleeping or looking as if he was sleeping.

Dalton had agreed with him not to make any unnecessary noises and he paced slowly around the perimeter, eventually passing by him, but he scraped his feet along the ground, raising enough noise to wake a light sleeper.

The lawman offered no sign that he'd heard Dalton and Dalton stopped in front of him. He looked down at him and smiled at his lack of attentiveness.

'Melrose,' he whispered, 'you awake?'

He waited, but received no answer – not even a low snore – and he dropped to his knees and shook his shoulder.

Melrose just rolled over, his stiff body thudding to the

ground and, as the blanket rolled with him, Dalton saw the revealed earth.

Wetness, inky and thick in the moonlight had pooled where Melrose's body had lain: blood.

CHAPTER 8

Dalton confirmed that Sheriff Melrose was dead. His neck's gaping second mouth had given the lawman no chance of surviving, and although he couldn't find the knife, he looked for prints leading away from the body.

He saw nothing to confirm that the killer had either left the ledge or returned to the wagons to sleep.

'Is he dead?' Loren said from behind him.

Dalton swirled round, his hand reaching for his gun, but Loren was standing casually and peering at the lawman.

'I didn't hear you sneak up on me.'

Loren slipped past Dalton and knelt beside Melrose. He raised the blanket, winced, then draped it over his head.

'And from the looks of this, that was Melrose's downfall. This is the work of someone without a conscience and no desire to face a man head on.' Loren rose. 'You want to tell me who you suspect?'

'Melrose didn't bring you into his confidence for a reason.'

'Then don't make the same mistake.' Loren spread his hands. 'I don't trust you and you don't trust me, but if you reckon I know more than I'm prepared to reveal, telling me what you know won't add to my knowledge.'

Dalton couldn't find a flaw in that logic and he swung round so that he had a clear view of Loren's face when he spoke.

'Melrose suspected that someone from this wagon train killed Marcus Wilcox. The Spitzer brothers are probably after us to get hold of the thousand dollars the killer stole off him. And the killer has now killed Melrose to stop him seeing Eddy and Tucker Malone.'

Loren's expression remained impassive throughout these revelations.

'I guess everyone will figure most of that out for themselves. But now that your plan to force the killer into the open has gone wrong, you got to come up with a different plan or more people could die.'

'I know.' Dalton shrugged. 'Perhaps we should turn back.'

'That's one option.' Loren considered Dalton. 'But I know that Eddy and Tucker knew John Stanton. Meeting them wouldn't be good for you and—'

'And that would be sufficient motivation for me to kill Melrose. But I didn't do it. I can't prove that, but I didn't.' Dalton set his hands on his hips and returned Loren's steady gaze. 'So, can you convince me you didn't have a reason to kill him?'

'I got the same problem. I didn't do it, but I can't prove it.' Loren raised his eyebrows. 'The only difference is, I didn't have a motive to stop him seeing the Malone brothers.'

'That I know of.'

Loren's gaze flickered with a sudden emotion, but

104

Dalton couldn't tell what it was and he blinked it away. Then the two men stared at each other, but as neither offered anything more, they headed to the wagons.

Loren located a tin plate and beat it on the ground until he roused a group of bleary-eyed and complaining people, who looked at the dark sky, shivered, then complained some more. But they soon quietened when Dalton relayed the bad news.

'Sheriff Melrose is dead,' he reported, 'murdered, and somebody from this wagon train killed him.'

The hubbub this revelation raised continued for some time but when Melrose's body had been confirmed dead, Virgil called for a meeting.

Everyone sat in the centre of the ledge and voiced their concern about what had happened, but nobody was as worried about who had killed Melrose as they were about what they should do next. Newell summed up the general mood for resolving this practical matter.

'This mean we have to turn back?' he asked.

'It sure doesn't,' Virgil said. 'We'll bury him. Then we'll keep going.'

Newell looked away as Virgil glared at him, but Virgil continued to glare, confirming he wouldn't voice an objection, then looked at each person in turn, receiving several nods but no headshakes. His gaze ended at Dalton.

'But I still assume,' Dalton said, 'that one of us will head back to Applegate.'

Dalton heard Loren snort as Virgil raised his eyebrows.

'There's no need.'

'A lawman's died and we can't just let those prospectors know what happened. It might be months before they meet anyone else.'

'We ain't even telling them.'

Murmurs grew around the group as everyone looked at each other, but Dalton voiced their concern.

'You can't *not* tell anyone.'

'I can. We've come here to make our own rules and live our lives the way we want to live them. We take care of our own and don't need no interference from anyone.'

'A death of an innocent man is where we have to accept interference.'

'You don't have a say in this. You're only with us until we reach our destination.' Virgil gestured around the group, his hand studiously avoiding picking out Dalton and Loren. 'We accept what we want to accept.'

'You can, but Melrose died from a knife slash across the throat while he slept.' Dalton stood and set his hands on his hips. 'So, I sure ain't risking going to sleep if that's what you're prepared to accept.'

'I trust my people. His killer doesn't have to be anyone I'm leading.'

Dalton looked up the short distance of visible canyon-side above them, then edged to the side to peer into the dark at the remaining drop down.

'If Melrose had died anywhere but here I'd have agreed, but we're in the one place where nobody can sneak up on us. Whoever killed Sheriff Melrose is amongst us and we got to face up to that.'

'And we will. But you didn't get my meaning. I said the killer doesn't have to be one of us.' Virgil flashed a smile without warmth. 'I trust every person here, but two people joined us and—'

'Hey!' Loren shouted stepping forward and joining the debate for the first time. 'You can't accuse me of that.'

'Like Loren said,' Dalton said, 'hey!'

As several people voiced support for Dalton and Loren, that support gathering momentum, Virgil raised his hands, calling for calm, then looked at each man in turn.

'I didn't accuse either of you. I was just stating a possibility.'

'You were. Don't state it again.'

Virgil glared at Dalton, then shrugged.

'I will when the time is right. In our new life, we'll make our own justice and we'll work out amongst ourselves who killed Melrose. Then we will deal with the problem ourselves, but we don't need outside help.'

As this was close to the philosophy Loren had championed earlier, Dalton glanced at Loren, who stepped forward.

'Fine sentiments,' he said. 'But for that to work, you must have a clear idea as to how you'll unearth the truth. So, do you?'

Virgil's eyes flickered with momentary doubt before his usual impassive expression returned.

'That is my concern, not yours.'

'As John Stanton said, if we're to trust each other sufficiently to get a good night's sleep, knowing what you plan to do is very much everyone's concern. I ask again, how will you work out who killed Melrose without outside help?'

Murmured support drifted round the group, as Virgil remained quiet. Dalton glanced at Newell, wondering if he'd step forward with a reasonable argument as to how they should proceed. He had been the first to voice Dalton's suggested policy of turning back and seeking help. But he just stared at a spot before his feet, his furrowed brow suggesting that many thoughts were racing through his mind, but not ones he wished to voice.

At last, when the people who had dared to express their concern had silenced, Virgil spoke up.

'Don't worry. Remember this – guilty people always slip up. This evil person will not keep his crime hidden from the honest gazes of our good people for long.' Virgil bored his gaze into Loren, then moved on to look at each person in turn. Many people looked away and Dalton almost expected someone to blurt out a confession under his resolute gaze, but when he'd traversed the group, he pointed down the canyon side. 'But for now, we must put this tragedy aside, as we have put others, and face our next challenge of getting to the bottom of the canyon.'

'I say we don't do that,' Dalton said, his being the only voice raised in objection.

Virgil turned to glare at Dalton.

'Why?'

'Last time, most people went down in groups on the wagons. Can any of us trust the others enough to be alone with a potential killer suspended hundreds of feet above the ground?'

'I can,' Virgil snapped, giving Dalton's question no chance of gathering support. He lowered his voice, his tone a mixture of sarcasm and accusation. 'I'll even accompany you if you're that worried.'

Virgil's comment could have many meanings and to Dalton it almost sounded like a confession. Dalton narrowed his eyes.

'I'd prefer to sort this out before we risk our lives.'

'We can't do that, and I won't let you tear this group apart with suspicion and fear. We will carry on as normal and wait for whoever did this to expose himself.'

And with that statement of intent, Virgil slapped his legs and stood up, effectively ending the debate and drawing everyone's attention to the fact that first light was brushing the horizon.

The meeting broke up as the group prepared to head down to the bottom of the canyon. Only Loren remained to stand with Dalton.

He looked at him, his eyes hooded and his jaw firm, suggesting he'd heard something that had helped him form a suspicion, then he joined the others.

Despite Virgil's proclamation that the group shouldn't be suspicious of each other, Dalton noted that everybody eyed everyone else during their preparations to move down. And, once they'd buried Melrose, just about everyone inspected the rope and frame as if they might find a fatal flaw in the arrangement.

As had happened the last time, Virgil volunteered his own wagon to go down first. Even more than the first time, this act helped to stem the tide of growing concern, and afterwards everyone appeared shame-faced at doubting the others. A new sense of getting the job done took over and they started acting as a group again.

As they wanted to observe everyone, Dalton and Loren didn't volunteer to go down on foot to await the wagons and, as the route to the bottom was easier to negotiate than yesterday's, two other men went down.

But now that the wagon lowering was under way, Dalton didn't see anybody acting oddly. And even that curious dismissal of past misfortune that he'd noticed after Eliza's attempted kidnapping, and which had been admirable then, was repeated with Melrose's murder not being referred to again.

One by one the wagons disappeared over the side and reached the bottom safely until they'd reduced the remaining task to just three wagons. Newell insisted that Eliza go down with Henry on the next wagon, but that he should stay back.

And then, aside from the horses, Virgil, Jacob and Newell were the only ones left for Dalton and Loren to observe. As Jacob and Virgil drew up the rope after Henry's wagon had been unhitched below, Newell joined Dalton and Loren.

'The Wades?' he said, without preamble, his expression and posture relaxed, as if he'd come over to discuss a minor matter.

'That's my assumption,' Dalton said.

'I'm keeping an open mind,' Loren said.

Newell swung round to watch Jacob and Virgil. Jacob happened to glance their way, then snapped his head around as if he'd realized he'd been seen looking at them.

'What makes you think that,' Dalton said, 'aside from the fact you don't like them?'

Newell snorted. 'Nothing.'

Loren patted Newell's back. 'I admire your honesty, but we need more if we're to voice a suspicion openly.'

Newell's jaw twitched, perhaps as he suppressed an urge to mention a real reason why he suspected the Wades, then he gave a curt nod.

'You're right. I'll go down with Jacob on the next wagon. I have some questions I'd like to ask him alone.' He glanced at Loren, then at Dalton. 'Perhaps you might have something you'd like to ask Virgil while you're up here alone.'

Loren didn't reply. He walked away to help hitch up the next wagon, but Dalton stayed back to give Newell a grim smile and a nod. Then they all moved back to the edge, but when the next wagon was secure and Newell suggested his plan, Jacob flared his eyes.

'I will not go down with you,' he said, then folded his arms.

'Do not accuse me,' Newell snapped, pointing at him.

'Newell,' Virgil urged, 'you will avoid talk like that.'

As Newell grunted his irritation, Jacob shook his head.

'This ain't got nothing to do with Melrose's murder,' Jacob said. 'I just don't want to go down with a Boone.'

'That ain't right,' Newell muttered, his eyes flaring. 'Because we all know there's one of us you—'

'Newell,' Virgil shouted, cutting him off, 'this is not the time to air disputes. Right now, we have to get the wagons to the bottom safely.'

'Then stand up to your son for once and maybe there won't be so many disputes.'

Virgil snorted his breath, but then glanced at Jacob and, with a short nudge of the head, ordered him to get in the wagon, then he shook his head at Newell.

Jacob smirked as if he'd won an important point of principle. He sat in the wagon with his legs dangling over the backboard. He glanced around, his grin showing that he wasn't afraid of the height and that he was even enjoying the thrill of being lowered down the canyon.

He was still smirking when he disappeared from view, and Newell didn't mention the matter again as they lowered the wagon.

When that wagon had reached the bottom and they'd dragged up the rope, Loren considered the sullen Newell, then faced Virgil.

'And who should go down in the last wagon?' he asked.

Dalton caught the sarcasm in his tone, as there was no need for any of them to accompany the wagon. Earlier, several other people who were confident of their ability to negotiate the slippery canyon side, hadn't risked sitting in the wagons and had gone down on foot. And all the men here had stayed to the end because they could do just that, but Virgil replied as if the question had no agenda.

'Perhaps you and John should go down next and enjoy the view. Jacob sure wasn't scared about putting his life in other people's hands.'

'Then we'll do just that,' Loren said, his dry tone suggesting to Dalton that only Virgil's taunt had encouraged him to make that gesture.

Dalton didn't feel a need to make such a gesture, but Newell looked at him, his significant glance encouraging him to let him talk privately with one member of the Wade family.

So he joined Loren in sitting inside the last wagon to make the journey to the canyon bottom.

Inside, the weight of the belongings and furniture had been spread evenly across the wagon and, to maintain that balance, Dalton and Loren sat at opposite ends facing each other. But neither man felt the need to display bravado by looking outwards.

They waited quietly while Newell and Virgil checked the ropes. Then, with much creaking followed by a sudden lurch, they rose from the ground and swung out over the drop.

Dalton had no particular fear of heights, but after his recent fight with the Spitzer gang, he was pleased that the wagon was covered and he didn't have to look down as they dangled high above the ground.

The two men sat silently until the wagon began to descend in short drops. Then Loren smiled.

'We've watched everyone for the whole morning,' he said. 'So, who do you suspect now?'

'Still Jacob Wade,' Dalton said, 'maybe Virgil.'

'Getting all friendly with the family the Wades don't like ain't a reason to suspect them.'

'It might just be that, but you got to admit it was mighty odd that Virgil forced us to carry on and not fetch help.'

'It was, at that,' Loren conceded with a sigh, 'but I reckon he believes what he says. He wants to start a new life, free from outside pressures. He wouldn't kill to start that life.'

'Perhaps he wouldn't, but maybe Jacob would and, as Virgil would never accept that his son is capable of doing wrong, he'd act to cover up his crimes.' Dalton considered Loren. 'And your suspicion?'

'Newell Boone,' Loren said with a surprising amount of confidence. 'Marcus Wilcox was a snake-oil seller and Henry Boone is an ill man. Perhaps Newell wasn't impressed when Marcus's potion didn't work. He sure reacted when Melrose revealed who the dead man was.'

'Yeah, with surprise, as if he didn't know Marcus was dead.'

'Perhaps.'

Dalton shrugged, accepting that when people voiced suspicions, every action could appear significant. He shuffled across the wagon, then leaned out to look down. He judged that they were less than half-way down, swaying at least 200 feet above ground. Then he looked around until he located the outcrop of rock where they would meet Eddy and Tucker Malone. It was several miles away, so he still had time before he would have to find a way to avoid them. He drew his head back in.

'So,' he said, 'let me see if I understand our suspicions correctly. Virgil and Newell, the two people we suspect, somehow worked together to persuade us to get in this wagon when we didn't need to. And they're both above us and are in sole charge of the rope that's stopping us from plummeting to our deaths.'

'That's the situation.' Loren winked. 'But don't look so concerned. If one of them cuts the rope, at least while we're on the way down we'll know our suspicions were right.'

Dalton chuckled at Loren's grim humour, but try as he might to avoid it, he couldn't help but peer outside again to confirm that the descent was progressing safely.

Two doubled and crossed ropes were beneath the wagon and they looped up into a giant knot which connected those ropes to the main rope fifteen feet above the wagon, forming a tight canopy. All the ropes were solid and intact and Dalton ran his gaze up the taut main rope to the top where Newell and Virgil were out of his view as they controlled the horses that were lowering them.

He was about to slip back into the wagon, but then movement caught his eye and his gaze darted back to the rope above the giant knot.

There, two feet above the knot, twine had frayed apart and a length of that twine dangled free. Even as he watched, another strand spiralled away and, in a moment of shocked horror, Dalton realized what had happened.

Someone had already sliced through the rope and the

weight of the wagon was slowly splitting that rope.

Within seconds, the rope would break and they would both plunge to their deaths.

CHAPTER 9

Dalton darted his head back into the wagon.

'The rope,' he said, 'it's breaking.'

Loren stared at Dalton, his wide-eyed gaze drinking in Dalton's shock, then he joined him at the back of the wagon, their combined weight dipping them lower.

As they looked up, Dalton was sure the wagon jerked downwards and that the rope had frayed even more in the few seconds in which he'd been inside. The thickness of the rope was now less than half its original width.

He looked down, but it took over twenty minutes to lower each wagon and he reckoned they were fifteen minutes or so from reaching the ground.

The wagon lurched as the rope frayed again, convincing Dalton that they didn't have those fifteen minutes.

'We have to lighten the load,' Loren said, 'and reduce the strain on the rope.'

Dalton nodded, no other plan coming to him, and turned. Inside were the total belongings of a family and he balked at destroying them, but if this wagon plummeted that would happen anyhow.

As Loren grabbed the first armful, he shouted down

that everyone should watch out. Then he hurled the nearest sack out.

First, they hurled clothes down, ensuring they didn't hurt anyone with their unexpected actions, and Dalton heard people shouting below, demanding to know what they were doing.

Dalton stopped hurling sacks down for long enough to shout back that the rope was breaking. Then he looked up.

On the ledge, the shouting had attracted Virgil's and Newell's attention and they were peering over the side. From so far away, Dalton couldn't discern whether or not their expressions were shocked, but when the wagon lurched again, that concern fled from his mind.

Since he'd first seen the frayed rope they'd lowered by only a few feet, and more and more cords were breaking away on the straining rope.

'We got to start throwing the heavy stuff over the side,' he shouted.

'Agreed,' Loren said. He pointed at a cupboard strapped to a dismantled table, then lay on his back to kick away the side-boards so that they could topple it over the side quickly.

Dalton moved to join him, but then saw another length of rope fray and part, even hearing the snap and feeling the wagon lurch down another foot.

'Don't bother,' he said. 'We'll never lighten the load fast enough. The rope's going to break any second now.'

Loren lay on his back with his feet raised for a moment, then he hurried over to join Dalton and look up. He winced, then grunted his agreement and they both stared around, looking for a safe berth to leap for on the near-

117

vertical side of the canyon.

There were numerous protruding rocks, scrubby trees, and ledges where a desperate man could perch for a while, but the face was twenty feet away and too far for them to jump to. Dalton did notice that the falling clothes had persuaded everyone to move out of the way, but in looking down, his gaze alighted on a ledge, around five feet wide and ten feet long. It protruded further than any others and could both be reached from a wagon dangling beside it and be rested upon, but it was fifty feet below them.

He drew Loren's attention to it.

'The rope will never last that long,' Loren murmured. 'We got to jump for it now and trust our luck to grab hold of something.'

'I reckon I've pushed that luck too far already.' Dalton stood and swayed, then righted himself. 'We got to get to the rope above the frayed length.'

Loren looked up and although Dalton saw him shake his head at the likelihood of their having enough time to succeed, he stood and gestured to Dalton to take the lead.

Dalton grabbed hold of the nearest rope, then pulled himself up. But the combined effects of his healing injuries and the lack of purchase for his feet on the side of the wagon meant that though he put lots of effort into climbing he managed only to drag himself up a few feet.

He stopped using just his arms to pull himself up, and braced his feet against the rope. Then he began to make progress, dragging himself up the rope towards the knot and possible safety.

Below him, Loren watched his slow progress, then tried a different method. He tore through the cloth, then climbed onto the cupboard, gaining height faster than Dalton had. He swayed with his arms outstretched then leapt for the rope above his head and hung on, his feet dangling beneath him. Then he climbed, hand over hand, up the rope before his strength gave out.

He covered several feet in four swaying lunges. That brought him to a point where he could dangle beneath the knot. He swung from side to side until he looped a foot around the nearest rope, then, with his weight spread over two ropes, he climbed on to the knot that connected all the ropes.

He glanced at the fraying length of rope, shivered, then darted a glance downward.

'Hurry! You ain't got time to admire the view.'

'I am,' Dalton grunted as he dragged himself up another few inches. 'I just wish I'd used your method.'

'I had to see the wrong way to do it to find the right way. Now hurry!'

Loren leaned down as far as he could and thrust down a hand. But his fingers were still feet away from Dalton's hands.

'Get above the fraying rope. I'll be fine.'

'Stop talking and climb.'

Loren thrust his hand down another foot and Dalton dragged himself up another clawed handhold. One glance at the fraying rope convinced him he'd never reach the top in time and he decided to use Loren's climbing method. He let his feet fall away from the rope to dangle free, then swung himself from side to side, kicking up higher each time.

Loren shouted encouragement at him and, on the third swing, he looped a foot around the nearest rope and hung on, trapped sideways and unsure as to how he could use his new position.

From above, Loren directed him to get both his feet up, then to brace himself between the two ropes. Dalton did as ordered and that released some of the tension from his arms, giving him the freedom to walk his hands up the rope and gain height quickly.

He flexed himself, ready to walk his feet higher, but then a hand slapped down on his arm and tugged. Dalton suffered a terrible moment where he reckoned his weight would drag them both down, but Loren braced himself against the knot and lifted him.

Dalton lunged and locked his hands on Loren's shoulders. When Loren stood the two men scrambled over each other before separating and standing on either side of the knot.

Then the rope split, its end coming in a rush of bursting cords, deep snaps and sudden drops.

Both men leapt upwards to grab hold of the rope above their heads.

Dalton had a giddy sensation of the ground falling away as the wagon plummeted from him, receding into the distance, and he tore his gaze away to check that Loren was hanging on. But then he saw that the canyon side appeared to be falling away, too.

He heard the wagon crash to the ground, then closed his eyes, unable to work out what was happening. When he opened them he was rushing in towards the canyon side. In shocked horror, he realized that releasing the tension of the wagon's weight had sprung the rope back up. With only his and Loren's weight now on it, the broken rope was flailing wildly, snapping back and forth and hurtling them in towards the canyon wall.

Dalton had just a moment to prepare himself and then they slammed into the side.

They were lucky in that they both hit sideways, but the jarring was so great that it shook Dalton's grip free of the rope. He saw Loren also come free, but then he was falling, pressed flat to the side of the canyon and sliding down an almost sheer slope.

When the Spitzer gang had put him in this position, he'd fallen head first and had lost consciousness the first time he'd hit anything, but this time he headed down feet first and that let him slow his progress.

He thrust out his arms and legs, scrambling for purchase in the loose rock of the canyon-side. His foot caught and slowed him and then he was sliding again. A trailing hand grabbed hold of scrubby vegetation, which came loose, but slowed him again. Then he slid down over loose grit, throwing up huge plumes of dust around him as he scythed down, but again he slowed.

For the first time since he'd seen the fraying rope, he started to believe he'd survive the journey to the bottom. With renewed hope he remembered the ledge that had been fifty feet below him. He darted his head around, searching for it. At that precise moment he slammed into the ledge.

His legs buckled and his momentum lunged him forward and almost carried him on, but he diverted his motion by throwing himself to the side and, on his belly, he slid to a halt, half-on, half-off the ledge. He took a deep breath, enjoying his good fortune and the relatively safe position he was in, then he saw a blur of movement ahead.

The shouting he'd been hearing, and which he'd

thought he'd made himself, registered and he realized that Loren had been tumbling on broadly the same path. And he would reach the ledge in a matter of moments.

Dalton rose to his knees then jumped to his feet, his outer foot barely catching on flat ground. Then he sprinted forward and threw himself to the ledge with his arms outstretched.

Loren might have been tumbling but he'd seen the ledge earlier than Dalton had. As he reached it he threw out his hands and the two men locked grasps. And then they both pushed backwards, their actions uncoordinated but both trying to find purchase on the ledge and avoid Loren's momentum dragging them down.

With an ungainly scrambling and much kicking, they came to rest. Loren lay half-hanging over the edge with his chest on the ledge and his feet dangling. Dalton lay on his side with his feet braced against the rock face and his head dangling so that he looked down the side at the people below.

'No sudden movements,' Loren whispered beside him, 'and we can both get back on this ledge.'

'Wasn't thinking of doing any of those,' Dalton said, still trying to focus on his upside-down view of the world, 'but how are we going to get down from here?'

Loren rocked his head to the side to join him in looking down.

Other ledges and handholds were below them, but they were still over one hundred feet above ground level.

'I don't know,' he said. 'But whatever we do, we'll have to do it on our own.'

It took Dalton and Loren nearly an hour to pick a route

down the side of the canyon.

At first they had to trust their own ability to find ledges below them that they could reach. Several times they reached safe berths to rest up, then found that there was no route down from there and they had to climb back up and try again.

But once they'd covered the first thirty feet of their journey the people at the bottom were able to shout up about what was ahead and so help them pick the best route down.

Then they made quick progress. Dalton even began to enjoy the challenge of climbing down. But he didn't relish the encounter they'd have to face when they reached the bottom.

And as they took so long to climb down, Virgil and Newell had reached ground level by the time they scampered down the last ten feet to join everyone. They received many pats on the back, but both Loren and Dalton stepped clear of the support to stand alone facing the two men, one of whom had tried to kill them.

'Are you all right?' Virgil asked, his tone and staring eyes registering concern which Dalton, in his annoyed state, chose not to believe.

'Yeah,' Dalton said, 'your attempt to kill us failed and now we can—'

'I didn't do that. Believe me.' Virgil turned to Newell, imploring him with his wide hands to support him, but Newell lowered his head. 'Newell was with me the whole time.'

Dalton and Loren glanced at each other and, in Loren's burning eyes, Dalton saw that, like him, he was determined to get to the truth this time.

'It was one of you two,' Loren said. 'So, tell us your stories and I reckon we can figure out which one of you is lying.'

'Neither of us is lying. We were together all the time and neither of us cut the rope.' Virgil again looked to Newell for support and again Newell didn't meet his eye.

'Then perhaps it was both of you.'

'That,' Virgil said, pointing a firm finger at Loren, 'is your anger speaking. It's more likely that somebody cut the rope earlier—'

'You're damn right I'm angry. Now, tell me what happened!'

'Perhaps,' Dalton said, as Virgil shook his head, 'that *is* what happened.' He glanced at the wrecked wagon, then at the other wagons standing further away. 'Somebody could have cut the rope while it was down here with the previous wagon and Newell and Virgil were too busy finding reasons to argue that they didn't notice the cut.'

Newell looked up for the first time, his narrowed eyes and pained wince suggesting that Dalton's guess at what they'd been doing was correct.

'But who?' Loren said, shrugging.

'Jacob was the last person down before us. He could have done it before the rope went back up.'

Virgil snorted and waved his hands high above his head.

'If you're now saying it happened on the ground, anyone could have done it.'

'They could,' Dalton said, 'but at the very least you got to question your son.'

'And,' Loren said, 'search for the money Marcus

Wilcox's killer stole. Wherever you find it, it's sure to prove something.'

Virgil's eyes blazed, perhaps suggesting he would never accept comments about his son being guilty, but then he swirled round to present his back to everyone. Dalton expected him to refuse to take any further part in this questioning. He looked at Newell, hoping he'd assert his authority, but Newell didn't look at him and it was Virgil who eventually poke up. His voice was low and trembling with barely suppressed hurt and rage.

'I deplore the accusations you've levelled at my people. This is the sort of behaviour we are trying to distance ourselves from. When this is over, both of you will leave us and we will find Pleasant Valley on our own.'

'Sweet Valley,' Dalton said, 'you're looking for Sweet Valley.'

Virgil turned. 'We have never officially assigned a name to our new settlement and I say it'll be Pleasant Valley and I will lead my people there without influence from anyone. Is that clear?'

'It will be clear, but only after you've called for Jacob and we've heard his story.'

Virgil snorted his breath through his nostrils, then roared at the top of his voice, the sound echoing in the canyon.

'Jacob, come here and show these worthless people how the Wades stand up to groundless accusations!'

As the echoes faded away, Dalton couldn't help but notice that Virgil locked his gaze on Newell and that Newell still didn't meet his eye.

But Jacob didn't emerge. Virgil's demand was so strident he must have heard it and everyone looked around, murmuring and raising their eyebrows at his defiance. Virgil didn't call for him again. He stood with his arms folded and his glazed eyes refusing to acknowledge that his son was actually defying him by keeping him waiting.

As Virgil's jaw muscles tensed and his cheeks reddened, Dalton felt a twinge of sympathy for him. He now saw Virgil for what he was. He had many faults, but he wasn't a killer.

Virgil was the father of a wayward and now murderous child, who couldn't accept that his own blood could do wrong, but as the seconds passed and Jacob still didn't emerge, Dalton watched Virgil's authority seep away.

If Jacob were hiding in fear of the repercussions, nobody would trust him again. And every passing second only put further pressure on Virgil to admit something he could probably never voice voluntarily.

People fidgeted. The muttering grew. One person, then another, slipped away to search the wagons, and when they didn't find Jacob, others joined them to look further away, but still they didn't find him.

Soon, only the four men at the centre of this crisis were left standing by the wrecked wagon. Virgil stood with his arms folded and his chin high, no sign of panic in his resolute gaze. Newell's eyes were downcast as he failed to acknowledge the problem. And Loren and Dalton stood together exchanging significant glances that confirmed that they both now knew who the guilty person was and that their problems would soon be over.

People drifted further and further away in their search. A check of the horses found that one was missing, but it was only when someone shouted out that they'd discovered a second horse was missing that Newell snapped out of his torpor and joined in the search.

Dalton and Loren hurried after him, but when he headed into Henry's wagon they stopped and debated how they could best help. But they never got the chance to start searching, as Newell emerged from his wagon and reported his terrible discovery.

Newell had checked on his father, but his eyes were wide and shocked as he hurried over to clear ground and attracted everyone's attention.

'What's wrong?' Dalton shouted as people milled in.

'It's Eliza,' Newell said. 'She's missing, too.'

CHAPTER 10

The ten minutes after the discovery that two people were missing from the wagon train were fraught and frantic. Virgil emerged from his state of denial but replaced it with another form of denial and organized everyone into carrying out a systematic search of the surrounding area.

Dalton and Loren stood back and let him complete this sensible check, but Dalton did encourage Newell to tell them what he knew. Newell shook his head and led them into Henry's wagon instead.

Henry was shaking, a hatred of his position burning in his sunken eyes. He was a man who would once never have let this situation occur and he hated himself for his current impotence. In terse sentences punctuated with harsh bursts of coughing, he told them what had happened.

Soon after Jacob had reached the ground, he had slipped into the wagon where Eliza had been comforting Henry after the journey down. He'd slapped a hand over her mouth then tried to place a pillow over Henry's face, but Eliza had struggled so much that he'd relented and taken her from the wagon. He knew nothing else about what had happened and, despite his pleas, nobody had come to the wagon to check on him until now, that fact causing him as much pain as everything else had.

Presumably before kidnapping Eliza, Jacob had sliced through the rope, but Henry had no information to confirm whether this was true. With the distressed Henry then beginning to repeat himself, Newell beckoned for them to leave, but Dalton lingered.

'Don't worry,' he said, placing a calming hand on his shoulder. 'Everything will be fine.'

'It won't,' Henry bleated. 'I'm dying. I ain't got long. I can't do nothing. I need her. I won't see her again.'

Henry continued to ramble, his words becoming unintelligible. This time Newell urged them to leave with more determination.

The three men emerged from the wagon and, without consulting the people scurrying around, headed for their horses. Quickly, they mounted up and debated the quickest way to pick up Jacob's trail.

But in those few moments they received an addition to their numbers.

'You ain't welcome here,' Newell said.

Virgil shrugged and continued pacing to his horse.

'So, you've decided to speak your mind. But I don't care. I'm coming with you to ensure justice for my son.'

'He killed Marcus Wilcox and Sheriff Melrose. He tried to kill John and Loren and my father, and I don't like to think why he's taken my sister.'

Virgil stopped to point a firm finger at Newell.

'Do not accuse him without proof. I have had enough of the unfounded accusations against my family from—'

'Both of you,' Dalton roared, 'be quiet!'

To his surprise, both men did fall silent, but having

gained some control, Dalton found that he had nothing he wanted to say to men who put arguing over a family dispute above action when a killer had abducted a woman. So, he just glanced at Loren and the two men hurried their horses on without looking at the other two.

Dalton heard Newell trot after them and then Virgil chase after him, but, as both men stayed quiet, he concentrated on helping Loren find Jacob's trail. It didn't take long. Few people came to the canyon and two riders travelling together presented an obvious trail to follow. Dalton asked if the trail could be Tucker's and Eddy Malone's, but Loren pointed to the outcrop, some miles away in the opposite direction, then confirmed the trail was fresh.

The trail headed off down the canyon towards lower land and, in a brief and quiet conversation, Loren let him know that the canyon carried on for many miles. It would take many days before they came out on to the plains.

Again without consulting Newell and Virgil, Dalton and Loren followed the trail at a gallop. The other two men followed them, but kept their distance both from each other and the leading men.

Dalton glanced back to confirm that these were the only people who had joined the chase. He noticed that further back the settlers were getting into their wagons and were looking as if they were moving on. Then the land dipped and they disappeared from view, leaving them with just the two trailing and distrusting men following them.

'Well,' he said, turning back to look at Loren, 'at least one thing's come out of this – we two can start to trust each other.'

'Nope,' Loren said, turning to Dalton. 'I still don't trust you.'

*

For an hour the four riders headed down the canyon. The trail they were following remained clear with two riders heading down the centre of the canyon. The tracks were recent, but whether they were closing on Jacob or not, Dalton couldn't tell.

The group was silent, but from his companions' reddened faces and stern jaws Dalton guessed that passing time was not cooling anyone's temper and that the previous confrontation could easily flare up again.

Loren was the first to risk speaking. They had rounded a jutting outcrop of rock and ahead the canyon presented a long and straight section for several miles. The men placed their hands to their brows and peered ahead, but there were no untoward movements. As clear water flowed from a nearby spring and crossed their path, Loren called for a rest.

Nobody disagreed. When they'd dismounted Loren stood before Virgil.

'Now we've all had time to calm down, can we at least agree to work together to find Jacob and Eliza?'

'I have no trouble being fair with any man,' Virgil said.

Loren nodded and turned away despite Virgil's less than obvious acceptance, but Newell snorted.

'And what do you know of being fair?'

'More than Henry ever knew.'

'Virgil, Newell,' Dalton urged, but both men faced up to each other and were oblivious to anything but finding another reason to argue.

'My father led this wagon train with a lot more respect for others than you ever have.'

'Respect is just another word for weakness and being weak won't get us somewhere where nobody can come along with their nasty plagues and—'

Newell stabbed a firm finger at Virgil's chest.

'One more insinuation is all I need and I'll—'

Virgil batted the finger away. 'And you'll do what?'

Newell stood toe to toe with Virgil; a long-delayed confrontation between these men was just seconds away.

'This is the worst possible time for this,' Loren shouted at them.

Both men continued to glare at each other. Then they shoved each other's shoulders as they worked themselves up to trading blows.

Before that happened, Dalton turned away in disgust and took the reins to walk his horse along the length of spring water. Loren joined him and the two men left the shouting and sounds of scuffling behind them.

'This is ridiculous,' Dalton said. 'We'll never track down Jacob and Eliza if we can't stop arguing amongst ourselves.'

'And what do you expect?' Loren said. 'None of us trust the others.'

'We don't, but I expect us two to be sensible enough to put aside our differences until we find them.'

'And that's what the new John Stanton reckons, is it?'

'I reckon.' Dalton stopped and faced up to Loren. 'And I never knew the real John Stanton like you did, but I reckon that's what he would have done.'

Loren's snorted his breath through his nostrils and advanced on Dalton.

'Don't ever tell me what John Stanton would have done. You ain't worthy of his name and you never will be.'

'And you're right. I'm trying to act like him, but what I don't understand is why a man whom John Stanton called a friend won't look for the good in me and give me a chance. I've saved your life and you've saved mine and surely that's good enough for the two of us to at least not be enemies.'

Loren looked away, his eyes flashing, perhaps with hurt.

'Never say that again. Every moment you continue to call yourself John Stanton just helps remind me you ain't him. I'll give you a chance when you start acting like the man whose name you've taken.'

Dalton rubbed his chin, then nodded.

'In that case, I'll start now. You don't trust me, and I don't trust you, and neither of us trusts them two.' Dalton pointed at the squabbling Newell and Virgil. 'One of us has to start trusting someone, and that person will be me. So, I trust you.'

'Why?'

'You knew what the Spitzer gang would do, but I reckon you were just following your instincts and not using any inside knowledge.'

'That's right, and it's something John Stanton would have known without insulting me with accusations.'

'Yeah, he did have instincts.' Dalton glanced at the canyon-side, then at the ridge above. 'And now, I'll use mine.'

Dalton mounted his horse, swung the reins to the side and headed straight for the canyon-side.

'What you doing?' Loren shouted after him, but Dalton had had enough of dealing with and explaining himself to everyone. He kept going.

Dalton rode on to the side of the canyon, then headed

for a terrace between two rock strata that cut upwards and which he reckoned would get him most of the way to the top of the canyon.

From here, he could see Newell and Virgil down by the spring-water. Dalton's sudden departure had encouraged them to end their flaring argument and both men were mounting their horses to hurry after him. Loren had already mounted up and was trotting after him. Half-way up the terrace, he caught up with him and repeated his question.

'I'm doing what you said I should do,' Dalton said. 'I'm thinking like John Stanton. He wouldn't blindly follow Jacob's trail, always being one step behind his quarry. He'd figure out where he was going and get there first.'

'You got some idea as to what he'd do, but you're going about it all wrong. You won't prove nothing here.'

'Then leave me and find him your way.'

'We got to stick together. Even Newell and Virgil realize that.'

'Then I tell you this: if my hunch is right, you'll stop facing me down and accept me for what I am – a decent man doing my best in a difficult situation. And you'll accept that I didn't kill your friend and that you got no reason to look for reasons to hate me.'

Loren didn't reply. They reached the top of the terrace in silence, then switched back to head towards a second terrace. Below, Virgil and Newell were hurrying up the first terrace to catch up with them.

'I can accept that,' Loren said at last. 'But only because there ain't no way your hunch is right. You ain't John Stanton.'

Dalton stopped for long enough to acknowledge

Loren's acceptance and that gave Newell and Virgil time to catch up. Virgil wasted no time in reiterating Loren's concern.

'I'm just trying to bring this to an end quickly,' Dalton said, turning to continue on up the slope. 'I reckon I understand Jacob. He'll head up the canyon-side the first chance he gets.'

'I understand my own son better than you ever will,' Virgil said.

'Do you?' Dalton shook the reins and carried on, forcing Virgil to hurry on to ride alongside him. 'Perhaps you're more concerned with countering the accusation that he's a killer than to hear the truth.'

'Which is?'

Dalton glanced back at Loren, who narrowed his eyes, encouraging him to be subtle.

'Perhaps this is all a misunderstanding. Perhaps circumstance has forced Jacob into actions he wouldn't otherwise do.'

'Go on,' Virgil grunted.

'He loves Eliza and he wants to get to Sweet Valley to start a new life with her. And if he has to do that without us, he will. So, he'll head over the ridge and try to find a place for them to settle down. We need to get to him first before that love forces him into doing anything else he'll regret.'

None of the men argued with this viewpoint and for the first time the group set off with a shared purpose. Even so, Dalton glanced at Loren, who returned a slow shake of the head and mouthed that Dalton wasn't John Stanton and his hunch would fail.

*

The four men stood on the ridge, looking out at the land beyond. The journey up the side of the canyon had been easy. They hoped that the wagons had found an equally easy passage and so would already be looking out at this vista.

But after hearing Henry's vision of Sweet Valley, Dalton had formed a picture of the land beyond the mountains as being a green and lush landscape, filled with numerous places for his people to set down.

Instead, under the harsh afternoon sun, the ground was brown, hard-baked and unable to sustain life. Clearly, even if they resolved this crisis, this group's odyssey wasn't over.

Then they headed along the top of the ridge. The south peak that Dalton reckoned Jacob would need to slip by to readily reach the other side of the ridge was still several miles away. And they rode towards the peak while constantly looking out for anyone cutting across ahead.

But as they approached a sudden sharp rise Dalton began to feel that Loren was right and that his hunch would prove to be wrong. In an odd way he had been trying to live up to the name of John Stanton, a man he didn't know and could only understand from the reactions of others. And his impending failure provided the final proof that he'd never be worthy of that name.

Virgil was the first to voice that concern, slipping his horse nearer to the canyon's edge and pointing out various downward routes. And Newell even supported him, looking down and reporting that they could see for miles and Jacob wasn't visible. Loren said nothing, letting his silence and the apparent failure of Dalton's hunch say everything he needed to say about Dalton.

At last Dalton called a halt at a point where the land ahead became treacherous. He directed everyone to take cover behind an overhanging group of rocks, where they could look back over the previous few miles of the ridge and wait for Jacob to show himself.

'He'll just get further away,' Virgil grumbled, 'if we wait here. I'll go after him on my own.'

'He has my sister,' Newell said. 'I'm going with you.'

'You won't. I will never travel again with—'

'That *is* enough,' Loren said with quiet authority. 'We'll all find out whom we can trust soon enough. If Jacob is coming, it won't be long before he's here.'

Virgil and Newell snorted, their flashing eyes and bunched fists showing they were prepared to carry this argument on until they traded blows, but then they slumped down to slip into cover. And with that being the limit of the agreement they could reach, they waited.

A half-hour passed, then an hour, and Dalton felt the last lingering hope that his hunch would be right slip away. He could think of numerous things Jacob could be doing with Eliza while they waited here, none of them pleasant.

But then he heard something.

At first he thought he might have been mistaken, but then it came again – the steady clop of hoofs – and they were closing fast.

The men glanced at each other, conflicting emotions of irritation, hope and anger registering on everyone's faces, but then common sense took over and they shuffled down to await the approaching people.

And, from the loudness of the hoofbeats, they would pass close by, perhaps fifty yards away. Dalton risked a glance out and saw that there were two riders – Jacob and Eliza.

Jacob rode at the back, a gun drawn and resting on his lap. Eliza rode up front, her head held high and her back straight with defiance and perhaps some fear.

With his eyes, Dalton signified to the others that it was Jacob and Eliza who were approaching and that they should wait until they'd passed. Then he shuffled down. But Virgil ignored him.

Loren had seen the signs of his defiance more quickly than Dalton had and moved to slap a hand over his mouth and hold him down, but Virgil was already on the move. He squirmed away from Loren's questing hand and vaulted out from behind the rocks to stand clear.

'Jacob!' he yelled. 'It's going to be all right.'

Jacob swirled round in the saddle to face him, then shook the reins and hurtled his horse towards him, hoofs skating on the hard surface.

'Eliza,' Newell shouted. 'Get away!'

Eliza turned her horse but still glanced around, uncertain as to which direction to go. By the time Dalton had shouted at her to head away, Jacob had halved the distance to them and Virgil was running towards his son.

Newell rose and chased after him. Dalton shouted at him to stay down but he ignored him.

Virgil skidded to a halt and stood before his son's speeding mount, but Jacob swung it past him. Virgil still lunged for him, but missed and fell to his knees. Then he hurried after him as Jacob galloped towards Newell.

Only the presence of the rocks behind Newell stopped him from running him down. But Jacob drew his horse to a halt, then leapt from his mount. He caught Newell around the neck and knocked him over. Then the two men rolled across the stony ground, entangled.

They came to a halt with Jacob on top. He wrapped both hands around Newell's neck and bore down on him. Both Loren and Dalton trained their guns on them, but with the fighting men being so entangled, neither man dared to fire.

Dalton hurried out from his cover, leaving Loren behind him. By now Virgil had regained his footing and he reached the two men first, then swung round to stand guard over his son with his gun drawn.

'Stay away, John,' he ordered. 'It was always coming to this and now these two will sort it out.'

Behind him, Jacob lunged down with all his weight on Newell's neck, his face darkening and his eyes bulging as he threw every ounce of energy into squeezing the life out of Newell.

'Don't kill him,' Dalton shouted.

Dalton didn't expect Jacob to respond. He'd merely spoken to stop Virgil shooting him as he steadily moved closer, but Jacob snapped his hands up to leave Newell lying gasping and clawing at his throat.

'I'm doing nothing,' he shouted. 'This man did everything and blamed it all on me.'

Dalton spread his hands, keeping them away from his gun.

'Then let's talk about it, but in the proper way and not with guns drawn and you with your hands at his throat.'

'This is the only way. We're aiming to live our lives our own way and we'll deliver justice our own way.'

'This ain't justice.'

'It is.' Jacob rolled his shoulders and set his hands together, ready to bear down on Newell again. 'This man killed Marcus Wilcox because he made his father ill. Then he killed the sheriff to cover it up and tried to kill you to make it look like I was the guilty man.'

This version of events was so different from what Dalton believed that he was stunned into momentary silence. The only thought that came to him was to keep Jacob talking and keep him from attempting to strangle Newell again.

But then Newell spoke. His words came broken and gasping.

'Don't believe him, John.'

'It's true,' Jacob roared, then bore down on Newell's neck again. 'You tried to poison Eliza against me.'

Dalton broke into a run as Virgil swung his gun round to aim at him. A single gunshot rang out. Dalton just had time to register that Loren had fired and winged Virgil's gun away, then he brushed past Virgil and launched himself at Jacob. With his arms outstretched he piled into Jacob's chest, knocking him away from Newell and the two men rolled away.

Dalton used his momentum to keep the roll going, ensuring that he dragged Jacob as far away from Newell as he could. When they came to a halt the two men lay on their sides facing each other.

'I beat you,' Jacob said, grinning. 'She came with me.'

'Only because you kidnapped her.'

Jacob twisted and forced Dalton to roll with him until Dalton landed on his back with Jacob sitting astride his chest.

'I took her away from you.' Jacob clamped a hand on his throat. 'And you backed the wrong man.'

Dalton doubted Jacob could exert enough pressure to strangle him with just one hand and he glanced to the side to see that Loren was running towards them. But Virgil stood in his way and grabbed his arm. Then the two men struggled. Eliza had come to a halt and was now edging closer to them, but she was out of danger.

Newell lay on his side, gasping and fingering his throat.

Dalton accepted he'd get no help from anyone else and swung round to look up at Jacob. He grasped both hands around the hand holding his neck and strained, then levered it away, but Jacob didn't put up much resistance and instead lunged to his side. When his hand reappeared, he was clutching a rock, jagged and glistening.

He thrust his hand up then brought it down like a dagger aiming for Dalton's head. Dalton wrenched his head to one side and the rock parted his hair before it sparked into the rocky ground where his head had just lain.

Jacob grunted his irritation then raised the rock ready to dash it down again. He held it in both hands and took his time, aiming to bring it down in the centre of Dalton's chest in a pulverizing blow.

Dalton flailed his arms, seeking to gain purchase and buck Jacob, but Jacob settled his weight down and raised the rock high above his head.

Dalton still strained but his questing right hand landed on a stone. It was only as wide as two fingers but it was all he could reach and he hurled the stone overhand at Jacob's face. The stone brushed past Jacob's raised arms and smashed into his bared teeth. Blood sprayed, accompanying a wince-inducing crack of teeth, and Jacob flinched back.

Fuelled on by his brush with death, Dalton surged forward, rolling Jacob on to his back and crashing his head into the solid rock surface behind him. Then he wrested the rock from Jacob's hands and raised it high above his head ready to dash it down on his chest in the same way as Jacob had aimed to kill him.

'Don't,' several voices screeched from behind him.

Dalton almost ignored them, every stored-up ounce of anger at Jacob's actions since he'd joined the wagon train threatening to burst out and make him smash Jacob to oblivion.

But he lowered the rock and let it fall to the ground. He turned. Virgil and Loren stood behind him, each having hands on the other, each restraining the other man.

'I'm not like him,' Dalton said. 'I'd never kill out of anything but desperate need.'

'And you've misunderstood him,' Virgil said. He tore himself away from Loren, hurried to Jacob's side, and knelt beside him. With shaking hands, he raised his head. A deep spasm contorted his face.

He withdrew a hand. Thick blood, dark and sticky in the afternoon sun coated the hand, as Jacob lay with his head rocked back, still and sprawled, oblivious to the debate as to his guilt.

Jacob died a few minutes after his fight with Dalton. The fall on to rock had caved in his skull. He didn't regain consciousness.

Now he lay in the shadow of the rocks with his father standing over him in silent guard.

Nobody questioned Dalton's role in his death. He had been saving his own life when Jacob had accidentally hit his head and died. But despite the lack of comment, Dalton reckoned Virgil would think through the incident and it wouldn't be long before a different version of events formed in his mind.

As regarded proving who had killed Marcus Wilcox, Dalton reckoned the truth of that had died with Jacob. The dead man didn't have the stolen money on him, Newell wouldn't dignify his accusations by defending himself, and Eliza confirmed that Jacob had said nothing other than to claim that he was only taking her away out of love.

Newell quickly recovered from his ordeal. With Jacob dead the group decided to return to the wagon train. In a line, they trooped along the top of the ridge.

They rode at a sombre pace. They let Virgil ride up front, leading Jacob's horse with his body draped over its back. Eliza and Newell rode behind him, neither person speaking after Jacob's doomed love for Eliza had ended in the worst possible way. Loren and Dalton brought up the rear, but again, neither man felt inclined to talk.

They hoped to intercept the wagons further along the ridge. Although Dalton accepted that travelling quickly was inappropriate, he still hoped they would be lucky and find them before sundown. A night spent alone with this unhappy group would do nobody any good.

The sun was setting over the peak ahead when he caught the first sight of other people, but there were only two of them and neither person came from the train. They were riding towards them from the canyon, heading from the opposite direction to the way he expected the wagon train to travel.

The group halted and waited for them.

'From the look of that body,' one of the men shouted, 'you got to them first.'

Dalton and Loren exchanged a glance, both men shrugging.

'You seem to know what happened here,' Loren said.

The man nodded, then pointed at Jacob's body.

'We met the wagon train. I'm guessing that's the man who took off with the woman and that's—'

'It was not like that,' Virgil said, swinging his horse around and advancing on the two men.

Both men raised their hands and smiled.

'No offence meant. We didn't come to start no arguments. We heard there was trouble and we came to help. Just sorry we got here too late.'

Virgil turned his harsh glare on Dalton. 'Yeah, we're all sorry somebody else didn't get to Jacob first.'

Virgil continued to glare at Dalton, but Dalton was oblivious to Virgil's taunt. He'd realized who these men were and knew the question that was coming. And even after several days of considering his response to it, he could think of no words that would explain himself to Tucker and Eddy Malone, two people who knew the real John Stanton.

Tucker and Eddy looked at each person in turn, then glanced at each other, and Dalton could almost hear the question coming closer to both men's lips.

'We were hoping to spend some time with our old friend, John Stanton,' Eddy said, at last. 'They told us he was with you. Where's he gone?'

Virgil flinched, then pointed at Dalton. 'He's here.'

Both men snorted, then shook their heads.

'He ain't John Stanton,' they said in unison.

CHAPTER 11

Dalton could say nothing in response to the confirmation of his false identity, so his only option was to run, but he never got the chance.

Unseen by him, Virgil drew his gun and turned it on his back, and Tucker and Eddy joined Virgil in covering him from the front.

In short order, Dalton found himself disarmed and kneeling with his hands on his head and with Tucker Malone standing guard over him.

Newell and Eliza remained quiet and Loren didn't even look at him, but Virgil had no such reticence. He paraded back and forth, extolling ever wilder theories about Dalton's activities and working himself up into believing that a man who had assumed another's identity must have committed all the crimes Dalton had blamed on his son.

Tucker and Eddy broke into Virgil's ranting to ask Dalton the only question that interested them – what had happened to John Stanton?

And when Dalton gave them the answer that he was dead, Virgil pieced together the full circumstances of the incident back at the river that had put Dalton in this position, putting that situation in the worst possible light.

'He's this outlaw, Dalton,' he said to Tucker. 'He feigned his own death. He used your friend to escape from a lawman, then repaid him by killing both men and insinuating himself into my wagon train.'

'It wasn't like that,' Dalton said.

'And how can we believe you when you've lied to us for a week?'

Dalton carefully considered his answer, but didn't get the chance to use it. Tucker Malone loomed over him.

'All I want to hear about is what you did to John Stanton,' he said, aiming his gun at Dalton's head. 'And when you've told me, I'll kill you.'

Dalton ignored the gun and met Tucker's fiery gaze.

'And if you were John Stanton's friend, you'd know he wouldn't have wanted you to act like that.'

Tucker's stamped a foot. 'Don't tell me what John would have wanted.'

He threw back his hand ready to slap Dalton's cheek. Dalton flinched away, but the blow never came and he looked up to see that Tucker was now looking over Dalton's shoulder.

Dalton turned to see that Loren had dismounted and stood with an imperious hand raised.

'I knew John Stanton, too,' he said, 'and I'll tell you what he was like.' He paced towards the group to stand beside Dalton. 'He was just like Dalton, loyal, trustworthy, brave beyond reason, and always willing to look for the best in people.'

Tucker and Eddy glanced at each other then lowered their heads, but Virgil sneered.

'You knew John?' he said, intoning each word with heavy accusation.

146

Loren swung round to face Virgil. 'I did.'

'And yet you've never mentioned that.'

'I didn't, and for the same reason that's on Tucker's mind. I wanted to know what happened to John. If Dalton had killed him, I'd have killed Dalton, but I've spent time with him, seen the kind of man he is, and I know he didn't kill John. I doubted him, but now I'll speak up for him.'

Virgil swung round to look at Eddy and Tucker, but the two men were looking at each other. With brief grimaces and darting eyes, they debated what they should do in the way only people who have spent lots of time together can. They ended their silent discourse with a nod and turned to face Loren.

'You're right,' Eddy said. 'John wouldn't have wanted us taking no revenge on an innocent man.'

Tucker looked at Dalton. 'We'd be obliged if you'd tell us what happened and then we'll be on our way to mourn our friend.'

Loren held his hand out to Dalton, letting him speak first.

Dalton nodded and stood up. He lowered his hands to his side and took a deep breath.

'Like Loren here says, I was—'

'Loren?' Tucker spluttered, swirling round to face Loren. 'You're Loren, Loren Steele?'

'Yeah,' Loren said, his tone resigned and defensive.

'Loren Steele, John Stanton's oldest friend and partner?'

'That's me.'

'The Loren Steele who stole John's wife and destroyed his life?'

Loren firmed his jaw. 'I never aimed for that to happen,

but I guess I might have done that.'

Tucker and Eddy rolled their shoulders, their original belligerent stances replacing their resigned attitude.

'So, you're the man John talked about when we sat up in Blind Man's Canyon, drinking to past miseries.' Tucker snorted. 'And whenever he got down, he'd describe all the things he'd do to you if he ever found you.'

Loren sighed. 'I can't blame him for that.'

'And he ain't here no longer.' Tucker chuckled. 'But we sure as hell can do 'em to you.'

The group rode at a quicker pace than before across the ridge. Dalton and Loren rode together in the centre of the group with Tucker and Eddy's guns trained on their backs.

Despite his son's body on the back of his horse, Virgil was now in the mood to hurry. Eliza and Newell remained quiet, but Virgil made up for their silence by building up his case against Dalton and Loren. He twisted everything that had happened since Dalton had arrived, putting both men at the centre of the settlers' misfortunes.

With Tucker and Eddy adding their own low opinions of Loren, Dalton had no doubt that by the time they reached the wagon train the evidence against them would have reached damning proportions.

'So, you got secrets, too,' Dalton said to Loren when they reached a point where the ridge narrowed and forced the group to ride in twos.

'Yeah,' Loren said. 'But as you've said to me, don't believe everything others say.'

'I don't.' Dalton looked ahead. They only had another minute to talk before the group would bunch up again.

'Why did you really seek him out?'

'In short, she died three years ago, and I got to thinking he should know that and perhaps get a chance to forgive me, or beat me to a pulp.'

'From what you've said about him, I reckon he'd have forgiven you.'

'He would, and the fact he never got the chance meant I had to protect his memory.'

'And you did that when you spoke up for me. Implying I was worthy of John's name meant a lot to me.'

'Yeah, but you've been trying so hard to live up to that name that you've missed one thing.' Loren frowned. 'You weren't the only one trying to be like John.'

After that admission, they returned to silence and the sun was close to disappearing behind the approaching peak when they caught the first sight of the wagon train.

The line of wagons had reached the ridge, then headed down the other side for several hundred yards to rest up in a visible but protected spot.

The sight of the wagons subdued Virgil into silence as he led them down the slope. As usual when sundown approached, everyone was sitting outside in a rough circle within the wagons, a fire in the centre, but nobody so much as acknowledged their arrival.

As Eddy and Tucker so obviously had their guns drawn and a body lay over one horse, this wasn't surprising. Virgil stopped just outside the circle of wagons and dismounted, then signified that the others should follow and spread out around their prisoners. Then they trooped closer.

The circle of upturned faces and eyes bored into the group, but several people darted their gazes around. At first, Dalton thought they were trying to understand what they were seeing, but then he noticed that several people repeatedly looked towards two of the central wagons.

Dalton stopped and swung round to face one of those wagons as a man stepped into view from behind that wagon, a second man emerging from behind the other wagon.

Two crisp shots peeled out. Dalton saw out of the corners of his eyes that Tucker and Eddy hurtled backwards, their chests holed. Even before they'd hit the ground two more shots ensured they wouldn't get up again.

And then the two men paced into the centre of the circle. Although Dalton had never seen either man before, he was sure who they were – the Spitzer brothers, Fritz and Herman.

'You took your time,' Fritz, the elder brother, said. 'We've been waiting for you.'

'Yeah,' Herman, a squat and surly man, said. 'Now give us the money.'

'We don't have it,' Virgil said. 'Jacob didn't steal it.'

'Then that's bad news for you,' Fritz said. 'We've been tracking you up passes and over that canyon for a week and we ain't in the mood to wait. The only reason your people are still alive is because you were bringing the money back. Now, give it to us!'

Fritz glanced at his brother, who turned on his heel, then aimed his gun along the line of sitting people. His grin and frequent licks of his lips as he nudged his aim on to the next person showed that he'd have no compunction about firing and that he was just picking his first target.

Away from the circle, Dalton glanced at Loren, who spread his hands, rueing his unarmed status, then glanced at the bodies of Eddy and Tucker. The loaded guns of both men were lying beside their bodies, but to use them, they'd need a distraction, and soon.

'Which one shall I take out?' Herman asked, glancing at his brother.

'Pick one of the older ones first. Then we'll—'

'Stop this,' Newell shouted, stepping forward. 'Jacob may not have had the money on him, but he did steal it.'

Fritz darted round to aim his gun squarely at Newell.

'Then tell me where it is and you'll get to live.'

Newell stopped ten paces from Fritz, then pointed, his gaze resolute as he looked at Virgil's wagon.

'Search that wagon and you'll find the money.'

Herman and Fritz glanced at each other, then sized up Newell, their suspicious gazes hinting that they reckoned this was a distraction. In response, Dalton and Loren edged short paces towards the guns on the ground. But then Virgil roared with frustration.

'Do not believe that man's lies about my son,' he said. 'Jacob did not steal anything.'

Fritz licked his lips. 'Be quiet. We just want the money.'

Fritz grunted an order to Herman, who hurried into Virgil's wagon.

Again, Dalton shuffled a pace closer to Tucker's body, the gun just five paces away, while keeping his gaze on the other outlaw, waiting for a moment when he was distracted. But as clothes tipped out of the back of the wagon and Herman's annoyed tones rent the air, Fritz's gaze didn't waver from his steady consideration of the circle of people.

Presently, Herman emerged, tearing a jacket in two in his rage, and hurled the pieces to the ground.

'And now,' he roared, stamping his feet and drawing his gun, 'somebody will pay for that.'

'You sure it ain't in there?' Fritz asked, peering at the wagon.

'Sure am.' Herman's annoyed gaze centred on Newell. 'And you've just wasted my time.'

He raised his gun to aim at Newell, who stood tall, even puffing his chest and refusing to cower. Behind him, Dalton used the distraction to slip closer to the gun on the ground, judging that he might be able to reach it before Herman reacted, but Virgil surprised him by raising a hand.

'Before you kill him,' he said, 'you should take the money he was keeping from you.'

'We were trying to do that,' Fritz muttered.

'Then search Henry Boone's wagon. You'll find the money in there.'

'We are not spending the whole night following you people's orders. If we go in there, we'd better find it.'

'You will,' Virgil said, his voice calm. 'I'd stake everything on it.'

'You have,' Fritz muttered with grim assurance, then directed Herman to check out the wagon.

Herman kept his gun on Newell a moment longer then, with an irritated slap of a hand against his thigh, walked to the wagon. He climbed inside, muttering to himself about just what he'd do if this proved to be another piece of misdirection.

From inside Dalton heard Henry utter a strangulated cry, but then a louder screech of delight emerged.

Then Herman leapt down with Henry's chest held aloft, which he threw to the ground. He kicked away the town sign, pulled out a bag, which he ripped open, thrust a hand inside, then withdrew a bundle of bills.

'That had nothing to do with me,' Newell said, his tone bewildered.

'Don't care,' Fritz said. 'We got what we wanted.'

Newell looked back at Virgil, who stood with his arms folded and a smug grin appearing such as Dalton had seen before on Jacob's face.

'But I care,' Newell said. He fell to his knees, his hands coming up to hold his head. 'I've lost everything. Everyone will reckon I stole it.'

Twenty paces behind Newell, Dalton glanced at the gun to his side, but he was in Fritz's line of sight and judged that he couldn't reach it. To his side, Loren was nearer to the other gun, but, in looking around, he again saw Virgil's grin, an expression no man who had just lost a son should have even if he'd defeated the family he hated.

And that grin gave Dalton an inkling of who had killed Marcus Wilcox and why. He shot a glance at Loren, then set off walking towards the Spitzer brothers. Herman dropped the bag at his feet and swung round to join his brother in turning their guns on him.

'Stop where you are,' Fritz said, 'or die.'

Dalton paced by Newell then halted. 'I just want the bag.'

Herman snorted. 'We're not giving this up.'

'You can keep the money. I just want the bag.'

'What you mean?'

Dalton raised his hands then walked slowly to the pile of discarded belongings from Virgil's wagon. He kept his movements steady as he emptied a sack, then threw it to Herman's feet.

'Use that. It'll be easier to carry the money.'

Herman shrugged, his gaze incredulous, but with his tone guarded, Fritz directed Herman to do as Dalton had suggested.

'Why say that?' he asked, his eyes narrowing.

'And why are you interested? You don't care what happens to us now.'

'I don't, but tell me anyhow.' Fritz smirked. 'Or I take the bag.'

'There's something in the bag,' Dalton said, pointing.

'Oh?'

'Nothing valuable,' Dalton blurted as Fritz's eyes widened, 'but something that'll prove who stole the money, and we need that information to sort out our problems. After all, you don't want the man who really stole the money to come after you, do you?'

Herman straightened after loading the money into the sack. Fritz grabbed the empty bag, then tore it open to look inside.

'There's something in here that'll prove who killed Marcus Wilcox and stole this money, is there?'

'Sure is,' Dalton said using his most honest voice.

Fritz looked inside, then thrust a hand in and rooted around. His eyes flashed and he chuckled.

'Now, that sure is going to be a surprise to whoever—'

'No!' Virgil shouted, his face reddening as he broke into a run and pounded across the ground towards Fritz.

'Stay back,' Fritz ordered, turning at the hip to face him, but Virgil kept running.

The two outlaws didn't even glance at each other as they both fired, hitting the running man low. Virgil folded over the shots but staggered on, his momentum carrying him forward until he dived to the ground at Fritz's feet, a trailing hand thrusting out for the bag, but catching Fritz's ankle.

And then he rolled to the side, dragging Fritz to his knees.

Dalton broke into a run. He saw Herman swing his gun round to aim at him, but Loren had now reached Eddy's gun. A shot pealed out and tore lead high into his chest, wheeling him to the ground. And then Dalton was on Herman and rolling over his body as he lunged for his gun.

Fritz turned to him on one knee. As Dalton used Herman as a shield, he tore a shot into his own brother's body. Then Dalton slapped the gun on Herman's chest, sighted Fritz and fired. His single shot tore into his left shoulder and knocked him on to his back.

Dalton trained his gun on Herman but the outlaw was still. Then he swung the gun back up to aim at Fritz, who twisted round and stood up, then hunched over, ready to return fire. But the other settlers had reached their own discarded guns and the circle echoed to the sound of repeated gunfire as everyone worked off their frustration by holing the outlaw.

As Fritz's body twitched and writhed to a deadly crescendo of gunfire, Dalton hurried to Virgil's side. He was still breathing, but the outlaws' gunfire had ripped into his belly and Virgil was barely breathing.

Dalton turned away to see Eliza hurry into Henry's wagon, while Newell loitered nearby, perhaps torn between joining his sister and trying to resolve the family feud before Virgil died.

Dalton moved to follow Eliza and check on Henry, but

Loren hailed him. He turned to see that Loren had collected the bag and was wandering over to him, peering inside it. Then he tipped it up, but nothing emerged.

'It's empty,' he said, not sounding particularly surprised.

'Sure was,' Dalton said, 'but Virgil thought there might be something in it.'

Loren nodded. 'And he couldn't risk that that something would prove Jacob's guilt.'

'Maybe that is . . .' Dalton winced. Eliza was emerging from the wagon and she looked at Newell, her mouth framing the other words that Dalton had dreaded hearing since he'd joined these people. 'But we'll have to work that out another time. Henry is dying.'

CHAPTER 12

Dalton slipped his hands beneath Henry's limp body and lifted him from his bedding, the old man's weight no greater than that of a child's. His breathing was shallow and his mutterings were unintelligible, but Dalton paced out of the wagon, through the circle of people and away towards Sweet Valley.

Only Eliza and Newell hurried on to join him and they headed to a small outcrop where they could see the landscape ahead. Under the weak rays of the setting sun, the terrain beyond the ridge glowed with a deep redness, the panorama of ridges and canyons stark and uninviting.

'Show me Sweet Valley,' Henry croaked.

Dalton turned Henry round to face the barren terrain, but the old man's eyes remained closed.

'It's beautiful,' he wheezed. 'Make sure my people are happy there.'

'I will.'

'Tell me . . . Tell me. . . .'

Dalton guessed what he wanted and he started to describe an idyllic place where they would settle down, but Henry uttered a low sigh, then flopped. Dalton glanced at Eliza, who buried her head against Henry's chest, and

Newell rested a hand on his father's shoulder.

They stood there for a while, seeing the redness that had consumed the landscape fade to dull brown. Then they headed back to the wagons.

Loren was waiting a respectful distance from them. As he walked back with them he reported that Virgil had died.

With no family left to state the Wade family's needs, Newell and Eliza agreed that they would find a spot near by to bury Virgil and Jacob so they could watch over them for the rest of their journey. But both agreed that Henry wouldn't rest too close to them.

Fifty yards from the wagons, Dalton passed Henry's body to Newell. Then he and Loren slowed so that Newell and Eliza could lead the way. But when they were out of earshot, Loren confirmed that the family feud would continue after the deaths.

'Your bluff worked,' he said, holding up a letter. 'But it was no bluff. There really was proof in the bag. This had slipped down into the lining.'

'What does it say?'

'Virgil wrote to Marcus Wilcox. He paid him a thousand dollars to poison Henry Boone real slow.'

Dalton winced. 'That doesn't prove he killed Marcus.'

'Perhaps not, but I reckon Marcus wanted more money, or maybe Virgil had to silence him. Either way, he stole back his own money and hid it in Henry's chest when he visited him.' Loren sighed. 'It seems he hated Henry so much, he was prepared to lose his own son.'

'Sounds possible.' Dalton looked back towards Sweet Valley, then at the ridge. 'But that just leaves the question of what we should do now.'

Ahead, Eliza and Newell had reached the wagons and had placed Henry's body in his wagon. While everyone gathered around, Newell collected the town sign and they headed back to them, their heads bowed and their pace slow.

Loren shrugged. 'They're the only ones who know the truth about you, and me for that matter. I guess it's up to them.'

Dalton nodded and waited to face the people, who were now, by virtue of Virgil's death, in charge of this wagon train.

'Father made you promise something,' Eliza said, not meeting Dalton's eye. 'I hated it at the time, but it doesn't seem quite so bad any more. . . .'

Eliza looked at Dalton with an unspoken question in her watering eyes and, just like the first time Henry had mentioned it, the thought didn't sound too worrying.

'Maybe we can talk about it one day,' Dalton said, 'if I stay.'

'I hope you will.' She gulped. 'We need you to lead us.'

'We do,' Newell said, fingering the town sign. 'The last week has proved to me that Father was the man to lead this wagon train and not Virgil. But I'm not the right man either. Every time I had a chance to take control, I let it pass. There's only one man for this job, and that's you.'

Dalton pointed at the terrain beyond the ridge.

'But I have no idea about what's ahead. I can't lead you.'

'Yeah. You got no idea what's ahead, but none of us has.' Newell offered the sign to him. 'But that doesn't matter. A leader doesn't lead because he knows where to go.'

159

Dalton didn't want to take the sign, but Eliza and Newell nodded in encouragement, and Loren held his hand out, directing him to lead these people on the remainder of their journey.

'You didn't let John Stanton down,' he said. 'He couldn't have done any better than you have.'

Dalton sighed. Ahead lay a place where he could settle down and perhaps find the peaceful life he'd craved. He had promised Henry he would find that place no matter what the cost and no matter if his bluff failed.

And it had cost plenty and his bluff had failed, but he had no doubt that with these people beside him and with good friends like Loren to help him, he would fulfil the promise he'd made to Henry. And, seeing Eliza smile at him for the first time in a while, perhaps he could fulfil the other promise he'd made, too.

'All right,' he said. He took the town sign from Newell and held it aloft. 'Tonight, we bury our dead. Tomorrow, we find Sweet Valley.'